If she closed her eyes, she could still feel his touch.

His warm, steady hand cradling her chin. His feather-soft kiss on her cheek… Julie tried to forget the emotional closeness they'd shared, but it was impossible.

I'm concerned about his health, that's all this is, she tried to tell herself. But that wasn't the whole truth. She had so wanted Noah to stay with her, instead of leaving on his jet. She wished she had the chance to comfort him. She wished that when he was hurting, and when he needed someone to hold on to, he would reach for her.

But he'd gone back to his life in New York. It was a few minutes past midnight, which meant it would be three in the morning in New York. He'd be fast asleep, and in a few hours his alarm would go off and he'd start his day. It would be a day without her. A day where he wouldn't think of her once.

But she would think of him.…

W9-AKV-734

Books by Jillian Hart

Love Inspired

Heaven Sent #143
His Hometown Girl #180
A Love Worth Waiting For #203

Harlequin Historicals

Last Chance Bride #404
Cooper's Wife #485
Malcolm's Honor #519
Montana Man #538
Night Hawk's Bride #558
Bluebonnet Bride #586
Montana Legend #624

JILLIAN HART

grew up in a small rural town in Washington State, where she could ride horses and hike in the mountains any time she wished. Although she left home, went to college, got married and moved to the city, she is still a country girl at heart. When Jillian's not hard at work on her next story, she reads, stops for café mochas and putters around her rose garden.

A LOVE WORTH WAITING FOR

JILLIAN HART

Love Inspired.

Published by Steeple Hill Books™

STEEPLE HILL BOOKS

Steeple Hill™

ISBN 0-373-87210-0

A LOVE WORTH WAITING FOR

Visit us at www.steeplehill.com

Printed in U.S.A.

Your word is a lamp for my feet
and a light for my path.

—*Psalms* 119:105

To Cheryl McGee and Jolene Haskins—
extraordinary women, writers and friends.
The writingchicks rule.

Chapter One

"Noah!"

She was in his arms the second he'd stepped away from the crowded gate. Noah Ashton couldn't get over it. His little sister, Hope, married and glowing, flung her arms around his neck, squeezed tight and then stepped back to look him over.

Her brows furrowed and her mouth pursed downward as she scanned him from head to toe. Noah liked that about Hope, that she fussed over him. Not that he needed it and not that it made a bit of difference. She always had the same complaints when it came to his lifestyle.

"Do I meet with your approval?"

"You most certainly do not, and you know it, mister." She scowled, eyes flashing. "You look like death warmed over."

"I'm just tired, that's all. Long day, long night, long flight." Noah brushed aside her concern with a wave of one hand. "I'm good as gold."

"Gold is a lifeless mineral."

"Ah, but it's of great value."

"You know what I mean." She slipped her slim arm around his, steering him down the small breezeway in the tiny Montana airport. "You work too hard. Our grandmother is worried about you."

"Nanna hasn't seen me since your wedding. For all she knows, I'm still as good-looking as ever."

"Good-looking?" Hope's smile dazzled, teasing him right back. "There *is* something wrong with you, brother dear. You're delusional."

"Hey, women tell me I'm handsome all the time."

"What kind of women have you been hanging around? They obviously have terrible taste when it comes to men." Her dark eyes sparkled with humor.

Hope loved teasing him, he knew it, but he was a good guy. Did he deserve being hassled? "Hey, wait a minute. Not five minutes off that plane and you're torturing me. I'm a billionaire. I don't need to put up with this."

"You're only getting what you deserve." She winked at him. "You've hardly spoken to me since my wedding. I've been busy, but never too busy to talk with you."

"I've been overburdened with this takeover, and I figured being a newlywed, you needed time with your husband." Noah shrugged, not sure how to feel

about his sister's decision to marry. Good luck in marriage genes just didn't run in their family. "Are you doing all right? Married life agrees with you?"

"It sure does. Why, are you thinking about trying it?"

"Not in this lifetime." Noah swung his carry-on over his shoulder, steering Hope toward baggage claim. "I want you to be happy—don't get me wrong—but after watching our parents year in and year out, I still can't believe you're giving marriage a try."

"I'm not giving it a try. I'm in for life. And don't give me that look. Not every marriage was like our parents'." She led the way through the doors and into the crisp weather. "I never thought I could be so blessed."

She *did* look happy. She sparkled when she smiled. It was as if she'd found her heart's desire. Now there was a concept—the words *happy* and *married* in the same thought.

Remembering the chaos of his childhood, Noah shivered. If true love *were* possible, it had to be a rare occurrence—like a total eclipse of the sun.

Great that his sister was happy as a newlywed, but he wasn't about to be led astray from the path he'd chosen—a single, unattached bachelor's life. He wasn't about to wish there could be a woman out there who would love him just the way he was.

"Nanna is so excited you've come," Hope told him after he'd grabbed his luggage, and when they were weaving between cars in the parking lot. "It means so much to her that you'll be at the party tonight."

"I wouldn't miss it—you know that." Tenderness filled his chest at the thought of their grandmother. "How's she doing?"

"Fantastic." Hope pressed her remote key chain and the side door on her minivan slid open. "Getting married at her stage in life is an exciting event. She wants to make sure she does it right."

"And the engagement party is the kick-off event?"

"It's a celebration, Noah, not a football game." Hope stole his briefcase from him and set it on the floor of her van. "Tell me it isn't so, that you didn't bring work."

"Of course I did. You know I have to. I have a company to keep afloat while I'm here."

"Haven't you ever heard of a vacation? You know, where you leave your desk and phone behind and go someplace and enjoy recreation?"

"I've heard of it. Never tried it myself. Could be addictive and destroy my carefully guarded work ethic."

"No wonder you look like death warmed over. You really don't look well."

She'd hit a nerve, but he didn't want her to know that. Whatever his problems were, they were his. That's the way he was made—he could solve his own troubles. "I'm jet-lagged. Just came back from Japan."

"That would explain it. Okay, you're off the hook. For now."

He deposited his suitcase and garment bag on the floor. Now what? How did he tell his sister, who loved him and thought she was doing the best for him, that he didn't know about the state of his health? When he'd flown in from Tokyo last week, he'd spent the night in the emergency room.

He opted not to tell her and snapped the seat belt into place instead.

Hope negotiated her minivan through the airport traffic and soon they were pulling onto the freeway. The Christian country music on the radio mumbled in the background as the miles sped by. Noah stared out the window at the road ribboning between gently rolling fields. The rugged snow-capped mountains, dead ahead, rose up from the horizon to touch the enormous blue sky.

Peace. For a brief moment, the restlessness within him stilled. What would it be like to live here, spend each day absorbing the beauty and the quiet, letting serenity settle over like the sun from above?

Then his cell phone rang, and Hope glared at him in that sisterly way that said she was still worried about him.

Not able to tell her why he had to work, why there would be no peace for him, he took the call.

*   *   *

The church hall was warm and friendly despite the darkening storm outside, and the heater clicked on just as Julie Renton was stretching on tiptoe on the second-to-the-top step on the ladder. The crepe paper rustled as she pressed it to the ceiling. The air current from the nearby duct tore the streamer of pink from her fingers and sent it fluttering to the carpeted floor.

On the other end of the streamer, Susan Whitly cried out in protest as the end she was securing to the opposite corner popped out of her grip.

"Sorry." Laughing, Julie scurried down the step-ladder to rescue the crepe paper. "Doom strikes again."

"The more you say the word *doom,* the more it's going to follow you around like a dark cloud," Misty Collins called from the corner where she was draping the last of the tables with beautiful shimmery pink cloths. "Everything's coming along fine. We'll be done in time for the party."

"I can't help seeing disaster." Julie glanced around the large hall, already half-decorated thanks to her very best friends. "Granddad's had it tough over the past few years. Now that he's found happiness, I want this party to be perfect. To sort of kick off this exciting new phase of his life."

"With all the hard work you've done and the plans you've made, it will be beautiful," Susan assured her from high atop the other ladder. "Your grandfather is going to have a wonderful time."

"I'm praying that you're right!"

The party *had* to be perfect for him, Julie thought as she climbed up the rickety ladder. It wasn't every day a girl's grandfather got engaged. After being a widower for so long, Granddad deserved as much joy as he could get.

He'd been the only close family she'd had after Mom left.

"They say Nora's grandson is coming tonight." Misty smoothed wrinkles from the tablecloth. "You know, the really rich one."

Julie inwardly groaned. She was under enough pressure with this party going well. "I don't want to think about the billionaire."

"Why not?" Misty opened a package of lace place mats. "I mean, he's a billionaire. You know. With billions of dollars."

"That doesn't mean he's nice." Julie pressed the streamer into place. "Just because he's rich doesn't mean he's gracious or polite or even understanding about a party for his grandmother. He's probably used to events far more lavish than we could ever dream of. What if he doesn't think our efforts are good enough and isn't afraid to say so?"

"Julie, don't worry." Susan leaned the ladder safely against the wall. "This Mr. Ashton may be rich, but he's got to have a heart. He has to want his grandmother to be happy."

"What if he thinks my grandfather isn't good enough for his grandmother?" Julie's throat felt tight as she tossed the tape roll into the cardboard box she'd brought all her supplies in.

"Who knows? Rich Mr. James Noah Ashton the Third *was* on the cover of some magazine I was reading at the dentist's office. He lives a grand lifestyle." Misty argued. "I wouldn't mind some of that."

"Hey, I saw that picture and I thought he was to-die-for," Susan added. "He looked really nice. Like a real gentleman."

Hmm, a gentleman? Julie wasn't too sure about that. "Can you really tell from a magazine picture? Especially where they airbrushed away all his flaws?"

"What flaws? Judging by the picture, I don't think the man has one itty-bitty imperfection."

Julie sighed and didn't say a word. The indentation on her left ring finger remained from the engagement ring she'd worn for over a year. She definitely knew about men's imperfections. Specifically their unwillingness to commit.

"Maybe this Ashton guy isn't so bad," Misty argued. "Even if he does have blemishes or scars or something. His coming here to our little town, don't you think it's like a fairy tale? He could be my Prince Charming come to rescue me."

Julie helped Misty with the last of the candlesticks. "I love that you're an optimist, but believe me, I don't think Prince Charming exists."

"They do on my daily soap opera," she insisted. "Don't mess with my dreams."

Everyone laughed, even Julie. Okay, so she was a little disillusioned. She didn't mean to be. It had been a difficult year, learning to set aside her long-cherished dreams of a husband and children of her own. Her heart still ached.

Maybe someday her own prince would come, a man who wouldn't leave her, who'd never let her down.

It was a prayer, a wish really, and Julie knew deep in her heart it was one wish that would never come true.

The sound of the car door closing shot like a bullet in the quiet. Probably Granddad. Right on time, as always.

"Is that our promised pizza?"

"And our reliable deliveryman," Julie confirmed. "I'd better go help him. You guys stay here and put up your feet."

Cold wind hit her face, reminding her that winter was on its way. Soon, Granddad's wedding would be here, and she'd be celebrating the holidays alone.

But it's good for him, Julie reminded herself, and let the cold wind blow over her, chasing away the heaviness of lost dreams. She had friends, and she still had her grandfather, who was heading her way, awkwardly balancing a couple of pizza cartons.

"Julie!" he called out, his voice deep and robust, the way an old cowboy should sound. "I hope I got the order right. Good thing is they're still hot."

"You're my favorite granddad for doing this."

She ducked his Stetson brim to kiss him on the cheek, cool from the chilly air.

"Least I could do for the girls who are making my Nora's party special."

"Let me take these." She lifted the boxes from his arms. "Everyone's done a great job. The hall looks so nice. Do you want to come see?"

He looked sheepish—and a little panicked. "An old rustler like me dining with fine young women like you? Nope. Somethin' tells me I'd best be on my way."

"Shy, are you?" She tucked a twenty-dollar bill into his pocket and argued when he tried he give it back to her. "I'll let you get away with running out on us this time, because I know you have a beautiful woman waiting for you."

"Nora's grandson's gonna be there, you know." Granddad pulled his Stetson low over his brows. His mouth pressed into a tight, worried line. "Not sure how I feel about meeting him, though. My Nora puts a lot of stock in that grandson of hers. Thinks anything he says is as good as gold."

"Well, if he doesn't take one look at you and see what a decent, honorable man you are, then I can teach him a lesson or two. I didn't win state in calf roping two years in a row for nothing."

"That's my girl." Laughing, Granddad tipped his hat and backed away. "Wish me a bucket of luck, girl, cuz I'm fairly certain I'm going to need it. If I need help, I'll give you a call."

"You can count on me, Granddad."

"I know I can. You take care, now, you hear?" He climbed into his classic pickup and started the engine. He tipped his hat again as he drove away.

The church's side door swung open with a squeak. It was Susan. "Hey, I thought we lost you. We're some serious hungry women. I don't think you should keep us waiting."

"I've got the goods right here." Julie held the boxes level as she headed for the open door.

The warmth of the church beckoned her, but the cold kept hold on her. She wished she could do something to take away her grandfather's troubles.

She watched the red taillights of his pickup fade from sight. "They don't make men like Granddad anymore."

"Oh, there's a few good ones around. The tough part is finding them."

"Tough? How about impossible? I've been trying to find one to call my own, and I've given up."

"That's when it happens, you know." Susan held the door wide. "When you've given up all hope and you don't think you'll ever find love, love finds you."

Not me, Julie wanted to say, but what was the point? Susan had her beliefs, and Julie had hers. Three failed engagements that had taken more of her heart and her confidence each time she gave back the diamond ring.

She didn't have a lot of heart and confidence left

to risk on another man, another dream, another chance for happily-ever-after.

She'd make the most of the life God had given her—and that was easy. Look at all the blessings she had—a wonderful grandfather and soon a new grandmother, and lifelong friends she loved like sisters. What a beautiful life she had.

"We're starving," Misty called from inside the hall. "Is that pepperoni I smell?"

Because anyone holding a pepperoni pizza was popular, Julie hurried into the hall to share the meal with her friends.

Chapter Two

"Consider this fair warning."

"Warning for what?" Noah bounced in the seat as his sister navigated her minivan along the stretch of dirt that passed for a driveway. "Maybe I should see that this road gets paved."

Hope shot him a withering look. "Forget the driveway. It's been newly graveled. I'm trying to look out for your best interests. Nanna has her agenda."

"Believe me, I know. She hits me over the head with it every week when I call her." Noah squared his shoulders. "Don't worry, I can handle her. I'm bigger and stronger. I have a will of steel."

"Hey, Superman, I give Nanna two minutes before she brings up the subject of marriage."

"Marriage is like kryptonite to a man like me."

Noah winked at her. "One and a half minutes, I say. She's gotten pushy since she's become engaged. Wants to spread the torture around I guess."

"Misery loves company." Hope winked right back at him. "I can handle Nanna. She's not going to marry me off."

"We'll see about that." Hope brought the vehicle to a stop in the gravel driveway, beneath the shelter of a mighty oak. Rain sputtered from the sky, making the wipers skid on the windshield. "Did you want me to pick you up? Or are you taking Nanna to the party?"

"I have no idea. I'm just along for the ride." He opened the door. The cool and damp air rushing over him was enough to make him shiver as he stepped onto Montana soil. "Go home to your husband and kids. Thanks for the ride."

"Anytime."

He grabbed his bags and briefcase. His sister drove away, leaving him standing in the noontime rain.

The windows of the old white farmhouse glowed like a promise of shelter from the storm. The front door swung wide, casting a generous swatch of light onto the old-fashioned porch. Noah's chest warmed at the sight of the woman framed in the doorway.

"There you are." Nanna opened her arms wide, and he stepped into them. "I should have known my Noah would be here right on time. Oh, it's good to see my boy."

He hadn't been a boy in over twenty years, but he

didn't correct her. "You're looking as lovely as ever. I guess being in love agrees with you."

"And why shouldn't it? Love is one of God's greatest blessings and one day you're going to discover it for yourself. I've been praying, so you'd better watch out, my boy." She broke away and nudged him into the threshold. "Let me take a good look at you."

"I'm fine."

"Fine, my foot! Why, James Noah Ashton you look terrible. Simply terrible. What have you been doing to yourself?" Nanna shook her head, her mouth tight with disapproval. "I know what you've been up to, lying to me on the phone!"

"I wasn't lying—" He was being selective. He didn't know for sure if anything was wrong.

"Letting me think you're better off than you are! I can take one look at you and see that you've been working day and night, not getting enough sleep. Not taking care of yourself. Eating restaurant food."

"There's nothing wrong with restaurant food."

"Have you looked in a mirror lately? And why aren't you wearing a coat? Come inside out of this cold." She grabbed him by the arm and hauled him into her living room. "Now sit down and warm up in front of the fire."

She had every right to scold, he figured. And as long as she went on about his lifestyle, she wasn't bringing up the word *marriage*. He checked his watch. Two minutes and counting.

"It breaks my heart to see you alone," Nanna called from the kitchen, not sounding heartbroken at all. Oh, no, she sounded like a four-star general on the eve of battle. "I had so hoped you would bring along a date. It's not good for a man to be alone."

"I've heard that before. Somewhere, I just can't think where—" He strolled into the kitchen in time to see her wave her hand at him.

"Oh, you. Don't blame a poor old woman for wanting to see her only grandson happy."

"I am happy." He kissed her cheek and stole the oven mitt from her. "Move aside and let the master work."

"Master? You can't cook, young man." She chuckled, her laughter as sweet as a meadowlark's song.

"That's what you think. I bought this video series by some gourmet chef on how to cook. So you see, I can feed myself and I do know how to get stuff from the oven."

"Just be careful. The pan is plumb full—"

"I won't spill," he told her gently, because he loved her. Noah lifted the heavy pan from the oven and set her culinary masterpiece on the trivet to cool. The delicious scents of Italian herbs made his mouth water. "Hey, I just thought of something. You could give me the recipe and maybe I can make it when I'm at home."

"That I'd pay good money to see." Nanna squeezed his arm. "The lasagna needs to cool. Come sit down and I'll get you some of that lemonade you like. And no, I certainly will not give you my recipe. It has been a guarded secret in my family for generations.''

"Nanna, I *am* family.''

"When you have a wife and children of your own, then I'll give you the recipe. How's that?'' Eyes twinkling, she led him to the round oak table near the windows.

"Maybe I'll have to charm the recipe out of you because, face the truth, Nanna, I'm not getting married. Read my lips.''

"Oh, what you don't know.'' She tugged at his tie. "Sit down and relax. I've made up my mind to treat you so well, you're never going to want to go back to the big city and the job that's making you so unhappy.''

"I'm not unhappy,'' he reminded her, and because he knew he could distract her, took her by the hand and pulled out a wooden chair. "My grandmother taught me to treat beautiful women with respect, so here, have a seat. I won't take no for an answer.''

"There you go, charming me again. You're trouble.''

"Don't I know it. Now, sit.''

She slipped onto the cushioned seat with great resignation, but her eyes sparkled with pleasure. "It's so *good* to have you here. Now my engagement party will be perfect.''

"It's good to be here.'' He found a pitcher of lemonade in the refrigerator. "Tell me more about this man you're going to marry. When do I get to meet him?"

"Harold?" Nanna clasped her hands together. "Why, you're going to love him!"

Noah snared two glasses from the cupboard. "He must be quite a man to win your heart."

"He is! Oh, the plans we've been making. We've hired an architect and we're going to build a new home, can you imagine? It's a terrible big project, but oh, what fun I've been having. I've even decided on the house plan I want. It took a lot of looking, I tell you."

A cold sensation settled in the pit of his stomach. "Will you be building here on your land?"

"Oh, no. Harold owns a large spread. A simply beautiful place. The mountain views he has are a sight to behold. I've got a place for the house picked out on a rise, so we'll have views in four directions. There's nice afternoon shade for a rose garden."

Nanna's eyes sparkled with pure happiness, lit from behind. Noah hated having to ask the next question, but it was for her benefit. Clearly she was so much in love, she might not see this Harold's hidden agenda.

"So, what will you do with this place?" He said it casually as he set the glass of lemonade in front of her.

"Oh, I thought about renting, but you know how that is. I'd worry someone wouldn't take care of this house I love so much. Your sister has her own home and I'm sure as can be you don't want this land—'' She stopped midsentence and squinted at him. ''Do you?''

''You know I love New York.''

''I just knew you were going to say that. Well, you said it yourself, so I guess my only choice is to sell.''

''Sell?'' Noah didn't like the sound of that. ''Is this your idea?''

''And whose would it be? It's just common sense, young man.'' She took a sip of lemonade. ''Now, before you start, I realize there'd be taxes to pay, but that's your job, handling my finances for me the way you do.''

''But you don't want to sell?'' he asked carefully.

''How could I *want* to sell? I have wonderful memories in this house, but it's time to start something new for me. Maybe what this old place needs is a nice young family to fill these empty rooms. What do you think?''

''You'd make money off the place.'' A few million, Noah didn't add. ''I suppose you and this Harold have talked about that.''

''No, we truly haven't. We haven't had the time. With the new house and our wedding plans, I've been a busy bee, I tell you.''

Just as he expected. Nanna didn't suspect a thing. She didn't even consider that the Harold she loved could be a fortune hunter.

"Would you be using the money from the sale to build the new house?"

"Noah, you and that finance mind of yours." Nanna stood, and her chair scraped on the linoleum. Her hand settled on his arm. "I swear you've been working so hard and so long, you don't know how to take it easy. '…all our busy rushing ends in nothing.' My dear boy, stop trying to accomplish so much. When you're in this house, you don't need to prove anything to me. I love you just as you are. Perfect."

She planted a kiss on his cheek.

His heart filled with tenderness for this spry, lively woman who loved him without condition. As he loved her.

"All right, I know you're dying to tell me about bridesmaid dresses and colors of tablecloths or whatever it is you brides get to decide." He took her hand and led her back to the table. "Are you happy now?"

"Overjoyed." Nanna sparkled like a rare gem. "Sit and let me grab my books. I'll show you the picture of the wedding dress I picked only yesterday."

"I'd love to see it."

For his grandmother, he'd do anything.

Noah took a sip of lemonade, wishing it was a double latte, and watched his grandmother hurry from the room in search of her wedding magazines. Alone in the kitchen, with the rain tapping at the windows, a rare peace swept over him. A comfort so strong, he was sure he was doing the right thing, watching out for his grandmother.

The pink and gold decorations were airy and romantic. The glitter streamers winked like stardust. Candles waited, ready to be lit, and the fresh flowers emitted a gentle, rose scent that made the room a dream.

Julie took a final look at their handiwork and satisfaction filled her. ''This is like something out of a fairy tale. I couldn't have done this without my friends.''

''Your grandfather is going to love it.'' Susan put her arm around Julie and gave her a quick hug.

''Everyone is going to be wowed,'' Misty added. ''And speaking of impressing people, I've got to fly. If I want to impress the handsome, rich bachelor who's going to be in this very room in just over two hours, I've got to beautify. I'm wearing that blue silk swirly dress I bought in Missoula. It's the best thing I own.''

''Thank goodness I got my red shift dry-cleaned last week,'' Susan enthused.

Julie couldn't believe it. All this fuss over one man? ''Just because he's rich doesn't mean he's nice.''

''He *could* be nice. We don't know that he isn't,'' Misty reasoned. ''He might be a good dancer.''

''It's an engagement party, not singles' night.''

"It's a Friday night. There'll be a band. That means we'll have to dance with him."

"It'll be tough, but someone's got to do it." Susan looked determined to suffer. "My theory is that you never know what God has in store for you. In my case, why not a billionaire?"

Julie laughed, she couldn't help it. "Okay, believe Mr. Ashton is going to be your knight in shining armor. I'll make sure to introduce you to the billionaire. Satisfied?"

"Absolutely." Susan waggled her brows, looking full of trouble. "Maybe I'll get my hair done, too. Since I'm getting dressed up, it wouldn't hurt to dazzle him."

"Why bother? I'm sure Mr. James Ashton has his pick of beautiful women," Misty teased.

"You don't think he'll take a second look at me. Is that it?" Susan pretended to be offended.

"He could be looking at me instead." Misty flicked her hair behind her shoulder. "Maybe the billionaire likes blondes."

Susan and Misty laughed together, and Misty said goodbye. The outside door clicked shut as Julie snapped off the lights.

"I'll be back in an hour to direct the caterers." Susan grabbed her coat and purse from the dark corner. "Don't you worry about a thing. You just make sure your grandfather is here on time."

"You can count on that. Thanks, Susan."

"Don't mention it."

Together they turned off the rest of the lights and closed the doors behind them. The fat raindrops became a downpour the minute they stepped into the parking lot.

"I hope this is just a temporary thing," Julie called over a sudden gust of wind. "I'd hate to have to row people across the parking lot."

"Joke all you want, but it'll all work out." Susan shouted to be heard over the drum of rain as she headed to her car. "Drive safely."

"You, too!"

The sky let loose with a violent torrent of icy rain. Great. Just when she didn't think it could get worse… She took off running. Gravel crunched at her feet and rain knifed through her thin jacket. She flung open her truck's door and collapsed on the seat. With hands stiff from the cold, she found her keys and started the engine.

"Please, don't tell me it's going to be like this all afternoon." She flicked the defroster on high, but only chilly air sputtered from the air vents.

Rain pinged on the roof and streamed down her windshield. She shivered and swiped a circle of fog from the glass. Tree branches swayed violently in the wind. Twin beams cut through the downpour as Susan's car eased out of the parking lot and out of sight.

With her mind on the party, her grandfather and the billionaire showing up, Julie put her truck in gear and crept through the storm, keeping a close eye on the road.

* * *

"It was good to finally meet you, Mr. Renton." Noah shook the older man's hand. He hadn't found any obvious reason not to trust the man.

There was an honest glint in Harold's eye, that was for sure, as he grabbed his battered Stetson and headed for the door.

Harold may appear to be kind and decent, but Noah had learned the hard way that people were not often what they appeared.

"I'll look forward to seeing you at the party, son." Harold nodded in the way men from the country did, his drawl unassuming as he tugged open the door. "Looks like the storm isn't about to let up. Hey, that's Helen's car in the driveway. She must have just pulled up."

"Wonderful!" Nanna clasped her hands together, obviously overjoyed. "She's going to help me fix my hair. You drive safe, Harold, my love. Guess I'll be seeing you in a few hours."

"I don't see how you can get much prettier, but I'll be lookin' forward to it." Blushing, head down, the older man cleared his throat.

Noah blushed, too, realizing Nanna and Harold were waiting for him to leave so they could be alone. Well, he could take a hint. He headed for the living room to give the couple privacy.

Okay, so he sort of liked Harold. He was a well-preserved man, who spent his retirement running his ranch and seemed to love doing it. And the way Harold looked at Nanna—well, it *did* look like true love.

Don't jump to conclusions, Noah warned himself, pacing the room, listening to the fire pop low in the grate and the bushes scraping against the windows.

Trying not to listen to the murmur of his grandmother's voice in the entry hall, Noah whipped out his handheld computer. The little electronic notebook was his life support, and somewhere in the files he'd begun a list of everything he had to remember for today—

There it was. He scrolled down the list. Flowers. He'd forgotten flowers for his grandmother.

There was plenty of time. He'd just take Nanna's car and zip into town. It wasn't that far away. Hadn't Nanna shown him pictures of the bridal flowers she'd selected? This town, as small as it was, had a florist shop.

"Where are you going?" Nanna demanded when she caught up with him in the kitchen. "My friend Helen is here, and your sister will be by any second to help me get ready for the party. Are those my car keys?"

"If you let me borrow them, I'll bring you home a surprise."

"All right, then, fine. Take my car, but you be careful, young man. My Chevy is older than you are, so show her some respect. And absolutely no speeding."

"I'm not a teenager, remember?" He kissed her cheek. "I'll be good. I promise."

He said hello to Nanna's friend, pocketed the car keys and escaped out the back door while he had the chance.

The defroster in her pickup couldn't keep up with the fog. Julie swiped at the windshield with the cuff of her jacket sleeve, watching the endless curtain of gray rain that obscured the road ahead. What was that up ahead? She squinted to make out the faintest red glow flashing in the thick gray mists. Taillights. Someone was in trouble.

Julie braked, easing to a stop in the road behind an old sedan. She hit her flasher as thunder cracked overhead. Her pulse kicked high and fast in fear, and she reached for her purse, feeling for her cell phone.

There was no sign of anyone anywhere. Maybe the driver was hurt. Maybe—

A movement in the shadows caught her attention. The tall, broad-shouldered form became a man, rain drenched and awesome, as the lightning cracked behind him, zagging like a crooked finger from the sky to the top of a nearby knoll.

What was he doing out there? Didn't he know it was dangerous?

As thunder clapped, Julie bolted into the storm, ignoring the cut of ice through her jacket and the sting of rain on her face. "Hey! Get back in your car—"

Lightning splintered the sky the same second the man turned. The earth began to shake like a hundred earthquakes beneath her feet. As the thunder boomed like cannon fire, Julie saw it all in an instant. The bright streak of light overhead, the man leaping toward her and the spark of fire as a tree beside the road flashed with flames.

All she could feel was the steel-hard impact of his shoulder, the dizzying spin of rain as it knifed from the sky and the drum of cattle racing by. She hit the muddy earth with a breath-stealing thud.

Pain rocketed through her body and her head smacked on the rocky earth. The man's hand curled around the back of her head, cushioning the shock. Fighting for air, she was only dimly aware of the lightning and thunder, the cold and wet. The man's face was a blur as he crouched over her. A tree limb crashed to the ground at her side. Fire licked at the leaves, even as the rain made the flames smoke and die.

"Are you all right?" he asked in a voice as deep as night, as powerful as the storm.

She gasped for air but couldn't draw it into her lungs. Fighting panic, she knew she wasn't hurt seriously. All she had to do was relax—

"You've had the wind knocked out of you. You're going to be fine." The rumble of his voice was comforting as he lifted her from the ground and leaned her against his chest.

What a strong chest it was, too. Sitting up, Julie

felt a little better. Cold air rushed in as her lungs began to relax.

Thankful, she breathed in and out. She felt nauseated, but she wasn't going to be sick. Icy rain stung her face, the wind buffeted her and thunder hurt her ears.

"We'd better get you inside your truck." He took her hand, helping her to her feet. "You'll be warm there. I don't want you to drive, just sit and get your bearings, okay?"

Her toe caught the edge of pavement and she stumbled. His iron-strong hand curled around her elbow, catching her before she could fall. "I can make it."

"Good. I'd help you, but I think someone is in trouble. That's why I got out of my car." He let go of her hand. "You'll be all right?"

"Who's in trouble? What did you see?"

"All I know is that there's a horse with an empty saddle in that field. I was going to take a look when you pulled up."

"I'll come with you."

"I don't think that's a good idea." Lightning flashed the same moment thunder pealed. "It's dangerous. I want you safe in your truck so I can go help who's in trouble."

"Safe? Well, *you'd* be safer if you stayed in your car, too."

"I'm a risk taker," he told her. "A dangerous sort of guy. I don't need safety."

Thunder rattled the ground beneath her feet and seemed to shake her very bones, but it didn't distract her from the man's dazzling grin.

Dangerous? Oh, yes. He was handsome and confident and a complete stranger. There would be time later to ask who he was and where he was from. Right now someone might be in trouble. She scanned the field. "Where did you see the horse?"

"There." He gestured toward the far rise as lightning singed the air around them.

Julie could barely make out the bay pony in the downpour. "I know that horse. That horse wouldn't run off and leave his rider."

She took off at a run as the rain turned to hard balls of hail. Ice struck her like boxer's gloves as she raced across the field and over a knoll to the creek below rapidly swelling with runoff. The bay wheeled with fear as lightning and thunder resounded across the sky.

"Hailey!" Julie called, snaring hold of the gelding's reins. She couldn't make out anything in the gray and white storm.

"There." He spotted the child first, a small dark shadow on the other side of the creek. "That water's rising fast."

"We can cross it." Julie saw the gelding was in good shape and uninjured, but too panicked to ride through the fast-moving current. She tied him quickly to a willow branch, so he wouldn't injure himself further. He'd be safe, for now.

"Be careful," she shouted. "The water's rising and it's more dangerous than it looks."

The stranger was already at the steep bank. "Stay here where it's safe. I'm going in."

"No, wait!" Julie called, running full out, but the effects of her earlier fall held her back. She wasn't up to one hundred percent. "The current's fast—"

As if he didn't hear her or understand the danger, he plunged off the bank and disappeared beneath the muddy water coursing dark and deep.

Chapter Three

Knowing the flooded creek was powerful enough to knock a man down and keep him there, Julie grabbed the rope from the saddle and ran. She could feel her lungs straining—they were still tight—and air gasped in and out of her throat, but she pushed harder.

She wasn't about to let him drown.

The water pulled at her shoes as she secured the rope to a fence post. Her fingers felt clumsy as she tested the knot, but it held. The creek licked at the rope, sucking it out of her hands. She wrestled it back, held tight and leaped into the rising creek.

The shock of the water turned her skin to ice. Lightning flared so close she could feel the crackle in the air. Thunder crashed, rattling her very bones. Above the hammering hail, she heard the thin wail of a frightened child.

"It's okay, Hailey," she called to the little girl, but the wind snatched her words and tore them apart.

"Where is he?" The current pushed like a bull-dozer at her ankles, then her knees. He'd fallen in right here. Where was he? What if she couldn't find him? What if the current had swept him downstream? *Lord, please help me find him....*

"Toss me the rope!" a deep voice boomed above the roaring storm. "I can get across, I know it."

Julie stumbled. Thank God! There he was, climb-ing out of the water onto a snagged stump in the middle of the creek. The powerful current buckled around him. He looked muddy, soaking wet and blood oozed from a cut on his forehead, but from where she stood, he looked invincible.

Since she wasn't a blue-ribbon roper for nothing, she tossed the line, watching it uncoil as it sailed through the air and into the man's outstretched hand.

"Good throw!" he shouted. "Stay there where it's safe."

One thing about this stranger was really starting to annoy her. He was bossy, and she wasn't staying anywhere. "If Hailey's hurt, you'll need my help."

He glanced over his shoulder at her. Through the driving wind and thick hail, she could see surprise flash in his dark eyes.

Handsome guy. She didn't get the chance to think on that any further because the current knocked her feet out from under her. The rope held her as she kicked her way across the swollen creek. She surfaced just in time to see the big man kneel on the ground beside the fallen child.

"Are you all right, little girl?" His voice was kind, and it was amazing to watch how calm he was, how steady. "I'm Noah. What's your name?"

"H-Hailey," the child sobbed.

Julie secured the rope and dropped to the girl's other side. "Hi, there, cutie. What are you doing out here in the storm?"

"Miss Renton!" Hailey flew off the ground, burrowing into Julie's middle. "I wasn't supposed to be riding Bandit, but I didn't know it was gonna storm. Honest. He fell real hard. Is he hurt?"

"He looks perfectly fine to me." Julie soothed the little girl who'd been in her kindergarten class two years ago.

"Are you hurt anywhere, Hailey?" The man—Noah—leaned close, dripping mud and creek water on Julie's sleeve. "Tell me what hurts."

She cried. "My arm."

"Sounds like it's pretty bad." He leaned close, and even though he'd been at the bottom of a creek, he smelled wonderful—like an expensive aftershave, spice and molasses rich. "Let me take a look."

"Are you a doctor?" Hailey sniffled.

"No, but I broke my wrist once, so I consider myself an authority." Noah gently cradled Hailey's thin forearm and pushed her sleeve up over her elbow.

"Ow," she cried again.

"That could be a break. Look at the swelling." Noah's eyes met Julie's and there was concern in them. "It would be best if we can stabilize it."

"Just what I was going to say. We can use small branches from one of the cottonwoods." Julie cradled the girl in her lap, protecting her from the wind and hail. "Do you hurt anywhere else, Hailey?"

"Nope." She snuggled closer, whining a little in pain.

"Good. We'll get you home soon, I promise."

"Here." Noah reappeared with two fairly straight branches, stout-looking enough to stabilize Hailey's arm.

They worked together, as the wind strengthened and the temperature dipped. The hail turned to ice. Freezing wherever it fell, it turned the landscape to a white wintry world.

"Here, give her to me." Noah took the child in his arms as easily as if she were a doll, and tucked her beneath his jacket. Snug against his chest, at least Hailey would be as warm as possible.

The creek had risen to a dangerous level. There was no way to go around, so they went straight through. Noah held on to the rope, and Julie helped him keep Hailey out of the water. Julie fell once and Noah slipped, but the taut line kept them both upright. Exhausted, they made it to the opposite bank.

"Is there a hospital nearby?" Noah shouted to be heard over the fierce storm. "She's cold. Too cold."

"Her grandmother lives just up the road. We'll

take her there.'' Julie slipped and slid through the icy field until the pavement was safely under their feet.

She took one look at the sedan off to the side of the road, taillights flashing eerily through the thick white curtain of snow. ''Let's get her into my truck. I've got four-wheel drive.''

''Something tells me we might need it.'' Noah cradled the child out of the wind.

Julie yanked open the door, threw the seat back to grab a couple blankets stashed there.

''You get the truck started.'' He stole the blankets from her. ''We've got to get her warm.''

That was what she was about to do, but she didn't waste time arguing. She ducked her head into the wind, scrambled across the snow and ice to the driver's side, and turned the key in the ignition. The engine leaped to life and tepid air puffed out of the vents. Julie turned the heater on high. At least the engine hadn't cooled off completely—she was thankful for that.

Hailey's tears echoed in the cab. Wrapped in two blankets, shivering in Noah's strong arms, she looked small and vulnerable. But safe.

Julie smoothed the girl's tangled curls. ''You're going to be warm soon, I promise.''

''Want my d-daddy.''

''We'll get you to him, I promise.'' Julie tugged the cell phone from her purse and tried dialing. ''With the luck I've been having, I should have known this wouldn't work. It's the storm. I've got to scrape the windshield—"

She got out of the truck and slammed the door shut, not needing his instruction. Cold had settled like pain in her midsection and, being wet to the skin, she actually couldn't get much colder. As she dug the scraper into the stubborn frozen mess on her windshield, she fought the driving ice with each swipe. Her hands were numb and she kept working until she'd pried the windshield wipers free.

The truck was mildly warm, but she couldn't feel the heat or her feet as she pushed in the clutch. "Hailey, how are you doing?"

"Still want my d-daddy."

"We'll find him for you, don't you worry." With a prayer on her lips, Julie backed onto the road. She couldn't see much, but there were no headlights coming her way.

Everything she'd fretted over and worried about today was insignificant now as she clenched her teeth to keep them from rattling. She wrapped her numb fingers around the steering wheel and peered through the veil of white hiding the road from her sight.

All that mattered was getting Hailey home.

Over the rasp of the wipers on the windshield and the whir of the heater, Noah's low, melted-chocolate voice seemed to drive away the fury of the storm. He was talking to Hailey, assuring her that her horse would be all right, and asking her questions about the animal. What was his name? How old was he? Was he a good horse?

Hailey answered quietly in a trembling voice. As the minutes passed and warmth filled the cab, the girl stopped shaking and climbed onto the seat between them. She told how she'd been racing Bandit for home to beat the lightning, but he got real scared.

Out of the corner of her eye, Julie couldn't help watching the big man who seemed to fill up half the cab. He had to be well over six foot, by the way his knees were bent to keep from hitting the glove box. It had been something how he'd taken care of Hailey.

"I had a pony once, too," Noah told the girl. "I rode him to play polo."

"Polo?" Julie had to question him on that. "No respectable Montanan plays polo. Rides broncos, maybe, ropes calf, definitely. But polo?"

"I was only a kid at the time, so don't hold it against me. Now I like baseball. Do Montanans like baseball?"

"What kind of question is that?" She nodded toward the minor league cap on the dash. "Okay, so I won't toss you out on your ear, but only if you never mention polo again."

"You drive a hard bargain, Miss Renton." He winked at her.

With his hair wet and slicked away from his face, and his jacket clinging to every contour of his remarkable chest, he looked like a dream come true.

He's trouble, Julie. Big-time, one-hundred-percent

trouble. A sensible woman would keep the Continental Divide between them—and that's exactly what she was going to do.

As soon as she got Hailey home.

Heaven was kind to her, because she spotted the Coreys' driveway and eased off the road. The tires churned up the steep lane. No sooner had she slid to a stop in front of the carport, there was Mrs. Corey, arms outstretched, taking Hailey from Noah's arms.

"I can't believe you found her. Praise be, Julie, you're a lifesaver."

"Not me. I just did the driving." Julie gestured toward the strong man, holding the back door open for Mrs. Corey. "Noah here is the hero. He saw Hailey fall from her horse and stopped to help."

"No! Say you didn't." Mrs. Corey paled as she set Hailey down on the chair in front of the pellet stove and turned to stare at the handsome stranger. "Aren't you Noah? Of course, I've heard of you. Goodness, won't this be a story to tell. Hailey, my girl, you're hurt."

Noah knelt down, carefully taking the wet blankets. "We splinted her arm just to be safe. She should see a doctor."

"I'll call my nephew. He's a medical doctor and he's out looking for this little one, right along with the others. I've got to run and get hot water started. Julie, be a dear and call them on the radio."

"Sure thing. I'll send someone after Hailey's horse, too." As she left the room, she smoothed wet locks of hair out of her face and tucked them behind her ear.

A graceful gesture, and Noah couldn't look away as she crossed the room. Her jeans and sweatshirt were baggy and stained with mud from the creek.

She was no fashion statement, but there was something that made him look and keep looking. She was simply beautiful. Not made up or artificial, but genuine.

"Miss Renton's awful nice," Hailey whispered to him while they were alone. "She got a broken heart."

"A broken heart?"

"Cuz she had to give the ring back. A *really* pretty one. It sparkled and everything."

Hmm. A broken engagement, huh? Noah couldn't help turning his attention to Julie. She stood in the kitchen, visible above the countertops, where she was signing off on a handheld radio.

"Mrs. Corey, do you mind if I borrow your phone?" she called down the hall. "I've got to get a hold of Pastor Bill. I'm guessing that the party is canceled."

"What? You can't let the storm get in the way of an important celebration." Mrs. Corey marched into view, with a warm blanket outstretched. "Look, the snow's already stopping."

Julie Renton. Noah thought about that. She had to be related to Harold Renton, the man he'd met today.

The man ready to marry his grandmother and her money.

"I've got a bath running." Mrs. Corey tapped into the room and scooped Hailey from the warm chair. "We'll warm you up and get you into some clean clothes, and by that time the doctor will be here. Thank you again, Mr. Ashton."

"No problem, ma'am." He straightened. "Just make sure Hailey's going to be all right."

"She will be. Thanks to you and Julie."

Julie appeared, frowning. "Pastor Bill has promised to clear the walkways right away. I guess the party is still on."

"We'll try to make it, dear. You drive safely now, and thanks again." Mrs. Corey gave her a hug and, carrying Hailey deeper into the house, disappeared from sight.

"Did I hear her right?" Julie asked the minute they were in the truck. "Did she call you 'Mr. Ashton'?"

"Some people have been known to do that."

"Why?"

"Because it's my name."

The gleam of the dash lights showed the shock on her face. "You're Nora's grandson, the billionaire."

"True."

"James Noah Ashton the Third." She closed her mouth and put the truck into reverse. "What should have been my first clue? That you know how to play polo?"

"You're Harold's granddaughter, the one he kept calling his angel."

"I'm no angel. Granddad is just—" She wiped the fog from the rear window and backed up. "You wouldn't understand."

"Why not?"

"Because he's simply wonderful. And I'm telling you right here, if you don't treat him with respect, you and I are going to have serious problems."

"I'm not looking for trouble." He did his best to sound innocent. "Not unless it's already there."

"What does that mean?" She jammed the gearshift into first and held it while she eased out the clutch. "I knew it. This is what I've been afraid of all along. You're going to cause trouble because you don't think my decent, wonderful grandfather is good enough for a billionaire's grandmother."

"Where did you get an idea like that? I only want what's best for Nanna."

Only want what's best? Julie didn't like the sound of that. "Then you mean my granddad isn't?"

"That's not what I said. I'm trying to keep an open mind."

"Trying?" She popped the truck out of gear on the steep slope, gripping the steering wheel so tightly, her knuckles were white. "Tell me you haven't come to try to stop the wedding."

"Why would I do that? I won't break my grandmother's heart unless there's a good reason. If your grandfather is the decent man you say he is, there will be no problem. You have my word on that.''

Something troubled her, but Julie couldn't figure out what as she applied steady pressure to the brakes and turned into the spin as the truck slid. ''Then you're here only to help celebrate this engagement? You're not against it? You don't dislike my grand-dad?''

''I came all the way from New York just to make my grandmother happy by attending her party. That's all for now. You can't blame me for wanting to protect her. Aside from my sister, Nanna's the only family I have.''

''Then you understand how I feel about Grand-dad.'' Julie's blood pressure crept back down to normal, and she didn't hold the wheel quite so hard as she pulled onto the main road. ''All my life he's been there for me. Supportive. Understanding. Someone I could depend on. I don't intend to let anyone hurt him.''

''Then we agree.'' The deep lines etched in Noah's forehead vanished and he relaxed against the seat. ''No mother or father?''

''No. Mom ran off when I was in eighth grade, and three years later my dad was thrown from a horse and killed.'' She swallowed hard, but the pain after all those years was still there. Would always be.

''I'm sorry for your losses. That had to be tough.''

''With the Lord's help and my granddad, I managed to get through all right.'' She didn't tell him how lonely she'd been, living with relatives, always feeling as if she didn't belong. "Granddad's guidance made all the difference in the world to me when I was growing up."

"I know just how you feel." He nodded once, his gaze pinning hers.

She felt an odd connection between them. Suddenly the truck's passenger cab seemed to shrink and he was way too close. She was alone with one of the richest men in the country—probably on the planet—and he wasn't at all what she expected or what she would have predicted him to be.

"There's Nanna's car. It's a classic, she tells me. I think she's fooling herself because a refrigerator would be warmer than that heater she has."

Julie shifted into neutral and coasted to a stop. "If you want, I can give you a ride to her house. You're as wet and cold as I am."

"I'm tough." He flashed her a megawatt smile. "I guess I'll see you in a few. At the party. Save me a dance, will you?"

"Sure. No problem. I'll fit you in between the corporate raider millionaire I'm seeing and my supermodel ex-boyfriend."

He laughed, deep and rich, and there was something about him. He was like a flawless diamond and she was a cubic zirconia.

"Later." He'd meant it as goodbye, but it sounded more like a promise.

The door slicked shut. The fog and ice on the

windshield had completely cleared away, giving her a perfect view of Noah's confident, powerful gait. As if the cold couldn't touch him, he moved easily, without hurry, and stopped to fish the keys from his trouser pocket.

She waited until the car had started before she put her truck in gear. As she passed by, Noah rolled down his window and waved to her.

Her pulse skipped an entire beat. And why was that? she asked herself as she negotiated the icy road. What she felt was *not* attraction. She simply refused to be attracted. Hadn't she learned her lesson? Hadn't her heart been broken enough?

True love wasn't God's will for her, and she accepted it. Plain and simple.

As for that little skip in her vital signs, she'd simply forget it ever happened. She had a party to host. A grandfather to see married. For the first time in a year, she was standing on level ground. She was happy. She wasn't going to mess that up by wishing for a man who was out of her league.

Chapter Four

Noah turned off the ignition in the church's packed parking lot. *Lord, please let this engagement be right for Nanna.* He wanted nothing more than the absolute best for his grandmother, but with his opinions of marriage...well, what if she were making a mistake?

The possibility that she might sell her land and that Harold Renton, no matter how kind he looked, could strip Nanna of her sizable financial assets burned like a sickness in Noah's stomach.

Please, let this man she's marrying be good enough for her. Noah wished he could stop worrying, but since he'd accumulated his own sizable fortune, he'd learned how far ruthless people would go to get their hands on easy money. Even people who looked perfectly nice and who had perfectly nice relatives.

Sitting in the stillness of his grandmother's sedan, he felt no reassurances. Snow beat on the windshield and the wind buffeted the side of the car, driving the cold in. Even through the lacy accumulation on the windshield, he could see that the church hall was lit up like a Christmas tree, decorations visible in the windows.

It looked like the party was in full swing, and that meant it was about time for him to make an appearance. Luckily, he wouldn't have to stay long. He'd greet his sister, congratulate his grandmother and hit the road. There were a lot of women in that room, judging by what he could see through the window.

His stomach blazed with anxiety. Since his last romantic disaster years ago, he avoided most social situations. He'd learned the hard way there was no such thing as true love. He had his own fortune to protect.

Well, he couldn't sit in the car all evening.

A blast of cold air lashed through him when he climbed from the heated interior. At least the ice storm had tamed into a peaceful snowfall. White flakes tumbled all around him, accumulating quickly on the freshly shoveled sidewalk. His shoes slid, but he managed to make it to the door okay.

The chorus of "Blue Moon" drew him down the well-lit hall, and the warm blast from the furnace chased away the chill from outside. His stomach still burned. He decided to ignore it.

"Hey, stranger."

Heels tapped in the corridor behind him. He spotted Julie Renton closing in on him.

She tossed him that dazzling smile of hers as she looked him up and down. "You sure clean up nice."

"So do you." Very nice. She looked dynamite in an off-white gown with long, slim sleeves and a narrow waist. The skirt flared softly around her to skim the floor. Classic. "I've come with a peace offering."

"I didn't know we were at war."

"Maybe we should call it a limited skirmish. Over you wanting to protect your grandfather." He tugged the small plastic box from his jacket pocket. "I didn't know what was appropriate, but when I saw white roses, I thought of you."

She took the box in her slim hands. Surprise made her sparkle. "A corsage. I'm speechless."

"Lucky for you, no words are necessary." He opened the top of the plastic container and lifted the single rose, wrapped in baby's breath and a silk ivory ribbon, from its bed. He withdrew the pin. "Remember the promise you made me?"

"What promise?"

"To save me a dance."

Okay, so he was a lot nicer than she first thought. Julie couldn't quite look him in the eye as she held the collar of her dress so he could pin on the flower. It smelled lovely, sweet and soft.

It was perfect and thoughtful. She never should have judged this man before she met him.

He fumbled with the pin. So, he wasn't experienced at corsage pinning. Neither was she. She held her breath, aware of their closeness.

"This is trickier than it looks," he confessed with a lopsided grin. "There. I think that should do it."

She glanced down. "I like my peace offering. Does this mean I should give you something? Isn't that expected in peace time negotiations?"

"I'm holding out for that dance you promised me."

"What am I going to do with you? A man who brings gifts and likes to dance?" She slipped her arm around his, liking the friendly, solid feel of him. "I suppose I could agree to your terms, but it's going to cost you more than a flower."

"Fine. I can afford it." He opened one of the double doors. "Name your price."

"If you want to dance with me, then you also have to dance with my two good friends."

"Friends. I should have known." He didn't seem offended as he guided her through the room. "Playing matchmaker, are you?"

"Against my better judgment," she admitted, because it made him laugh again. "They begged and pleaded."

"I don't mind at all," he agreed pleasantly, scanning the crowded room. "You did a great job, Julie. I'm sure my grandmother is pleased."

That meant a lot, coming from the only billionaire

in the room. From the man who'd given her a corsage.

"There's Nanna." He nodded in the direction of the dance floor. "It's good to see my grandmother happy."

There was no doubt he meant it, and that he loved his grandmother. Julie knew just how that felt. Her heart ached at the sweet sight of her granddad and his grandmother swaying to the last chorus, gazing into each other's eyes as if they'd found true love.

True love. She knew from firsthand experience exactly how rare that precious gift was. She prayed her grandfather would know nothing but joy for the rest of his days. "They're a perfect couple. They light up from inside when they're together."

"They make you want to believe." He held out his hand, palm up, as the piano belted out the first strains of "Strangers in Paradise." "Remember our deal?"

"How could I forget?" She placed her fingers on his palm, featherlight.

A sharp sensation wedged hard beneath his sternum and stayed there. He ignored it, closed his fingers over Julie's and led her through the tables to the area in front of the band. It was hard to miss all the people turning in their seats to watch him pass. He tried not to think about it or the sharpness in his chest.

Just stress—that's what it was. He'd take a deep breath and… Pain pierced his sternum, as hot as fire and razor sharp. He missed a step, and Julie's grip on his arm tightened.

"Noah, are you all right?"

He was still standing, but he felt like a fool, so he kept dancing. "Yep. Just overwhelmed by my dance partner's beauty."

"Good try, but you can't fool me." Her fingers remained a firm presence on his arm. She squinted up at him, narrowing her pretty eyes, as if she wasn't about to be tricked by the likes of him. "You need to sit down before you fall down. You're breathing funny. Are you having any chest pain?"

"It's my weak ankle, that's all." He didn't want her to know the truth. "It's an old polo match injury."

"The fib would have gone over better if you'd used a baseball game instead of polo. You keep forgetting. You're in Montana now."

He rolled his eyes, pretending to be annoyed. "It's hard to forget where I am with so many Stetsons around."

"Not your typical Lower Manhattan attire, huh? Watch out. If you stay here too long, you'll be wearing a hat and boots and learning to ride."

"I'm heading back to New York first thing tomorrow morning."

"You work on Saturdays?"

"Sure. Got a busy week to look forward to." He was already starting to feel better. Maybe the pain was going to go away now.

She allowed him to pull her close—not too close—and whirl her to the Frank Sinatra tune. She'd almost made him forget the pain. Almost. It returned in a sharp lash through his chest, doubled in intensity.

Breathe deep. It will go away. At least, he was praying it would. "Really, I'm fine."

Julie froze in his arms. "That's it. Something *is* wrong. You look practically gray. You're sitting down. *Now.*"

"It's nothing to worry about. Probably just the clean air out here. I'm not used to such purity." I refuse to be sick. I'm not sick. *Please don't let me be sick, Lord.* Not at Nanna's party.

"You and your excuses. Unfortunately for you, I'm a teacher. I'm immune to them." Julie frowned and pressed her hand to his forehead. Her skin was cool and soothing. "I also have lots of practice with sick kids, so I can recognize the signs."

"I'm no kindergartner." Okay, now he was getting annoyed. "I don't get sick."

"Everyone gets sick now and then." With the way she bit her lip, she looked as if she was trying not to laugh. "Fine, have it your way. Come with me. *I'm* feeling sick."

Well, if she was feeling ill, he'd go along with her. "Maybe you need some fresh air, too."

"How did you know?" She was teasing him now, and he wasn't sure if he liked it. Miss Julie Renton seemed far too sure of herself as she hauled him out the back door and into a dark room.

"I'll be right back," she promised like the angel she was, disappearing through the door, leaving him alone.

The tightness in his chest was worse. Much worse. He just had to breathe deep. Relax. This was stress, that was all. It had to be. He was too young to have a heart attack, right?

Blade-sharp pain sliced from back to front, leaving him panting. He tugged loose his tie and popped the top buttons on his shirt. This is only stress. Just a lot of stress. So that meant he could will the pain away....

The door swung open, and warm air spilled across him where he sat on the concrete floor, clutching his chest. He saw Julie's eyes widen and the shock on her face, then the door slammed shut, leaving them alone in the empty room.

She sank to the step next to him and pressed a plastic cup in his hands. "You're not looking so good."

"Then I'm looking better than I feel." The punch was sweet and cold. It tasted great, but didn't do a thing for the pain in his chest. It hurt to breathe. It hurt to move. It hurt to do anything. He set the cup on the step behind him.

"I'm going to go fetch Dr. Corey." Julie's touch on his shoulder felt like a rare comfort. One he wouldn't mind hanging on to.

"No doctor." He cut off a groan of pain. Sweat broke out on his face. "This isn't anything."

"Sure, you mean, the way a heart attack isn't anything?" She slipped the tie from beneath his collar. "Let's get you lying down."

He caught her by the wrist, holding her tightly so she would understand. "I'm not having a heart attack."

"If you want to stay in denial, fine." She pulled a worn blanket from a nearby shelf. "There's a doctor on the other side of that door. I won't be gone a minute."

"Don't leave, Julie. It's not a heart attack." At least, he thought it wasn't. "It's some kind of stress thing. I've already been to the emergency room over this."

"Same symptoms?"

He nodded, pain hitting him like a sledgehammer. It left him helpless, struggling to breathe. He hated this.

Julie's cool fingers pressed the inside of his wrist. "You swear that you're not going to die on me?"

"Didn't last time."

"Great. That's comforting." She shook the blanket out and draped it over his shoulders. "I'll go get your grandmother."

"Don't tell Nanna." He choked on the words. The air in his lungs turned to fire. He couldn't say anything more. He couldn't tell her how important this was. To keep this secret from his grandmother. Please, he silently begged.

"What am I going to do with you if you have a heart attack on me?" She said it as though he was bothering her, but he could see the fear tight at her mouth. The worry furrowed lines into her forehead. "I should go get the doctor, call the ambulance and make them wheel you out of here."

"That would ruin my grandmother's party."

"I'm sure she wouldn't see it that way."

"I don't care. You're not calling anyone." More pain spliced through his chest. He leaned his forehead on his knees. His palms felt clammy. Just like last time.

He flashed back to last week. To being trapped in the emergency room, the monitors beeping, voices above him blurring, the ceiling tiles too bright and his fears too enormous.

The same fears whipped through him now. "Please."

What was she going to do? Julie knew she had to get him help. How could she go against his wishes? She understood exactly how important his grandmother was to him. "Can you make it to the parking lot?"

"I will make it." His hand found hers and squeezed.

She felt the need in his touch. Strong and stark, as if he had no one else to turn to. Maybe he wasn't used to relying on others.

She knew how that felt.

She helped him up. When he couldn't straighten, she almost pushed him back down. He needed a doctor. Now, not later. But he took one limping step out of her reach. He was one determined man. His back was slightly stooped and his shoulders slouched from the pain. His face was ash-gray.

The poor man. Julie grabbed the heavy back door before he could, and pushed it open. The wind roared in, snatching the blanket from his shoulders.

She caught hold of the wool and smoothed it back into place. A fierce desire took root in her heart, one she didn't understand. She needed to take care of him, to make sure he came through this all right. She'd give Misty or Susan a call and ask them to take care of things. The party would go on just fine.

All that mattered was this man at her side. The one who seemed so alone.

She knew how that felt, too.

Noah swore hours had passed, but he'd been watching the clock on the pickup's dash so he knew it was exactly seventeen minutes later when Julie pulled into the well-lit driveway. The red flash of ambulance lights glowed eerily in the snowfall. Pain seized him up so tight he could only breathe in little puffs.

Noah was dimly aware of a cold gust of air when she opened the door. She called out to someone by name, and the next thing he knew he was being hauled from the passenger seat and laid on a gurney.

He searched for Julie, but couldn't find her. Strangers' faces stared down at him as the world around him blurred and the gurney bumped over the concrete and through the electric doors. The ceiling tiles flashed above him like lines on a highway.

I don't want to be here. I'll do anything, Lord, if I can come out of this all right. I'll work less. I'll eat better. I'll take a vacation. I'll listen to my sister. I'll do everything my grandmother says. Just get me through this.

He knew he was bargaining. Pain roared like an erupting volcano in his chest, and he didn't know what else to do. He only wanted the pain to stop.

More strangers crowded around him. A needle pricked his arm. Cables tugged at the skin on his chest. Monitors beeped too fast, or it sounded that way. He worried about that, too.

We need to run some tests, the doctor back home had told him. But there had been meetings that couldn't be delayed, deadlines that had to be met and a business to tend to.

It was easy to put off a few tests, because a lot of people depended on him for their jobs. Jobs that made their lives better. That was important, and the attack he'd had was due to stress, so it was nothing to worry about.

Now he wasn't so certain.

As the people worked around him, grim and efficient, he had to admit it. Something was wrong. He couldn't deny it any longer.

"Your EKG looks good." The doctor jotted something down on a clipboard. "We need a few tests."

Relief left him feeling numb. That meant it wasn't a heart attack, right? He'd been fairly certain it wasn't—it hadn't been last time. But the pain had been so fierce, he'd started to wonder. It was probably just stress again. He would stop working on weekends maybe and get more exercise. That ought to take care of it, right?

A light tap of heeled shoes sounded on the tile floor near the door. Julie? He hoped so. This place was feeling lonely, and he wouldn't mind seeing a familiar face.

The shoes hesitated on the other side of the blue curtain, then a chair rasped against the floor. "Sarah," a stranger's voice said to someone else on the other side of the curtain on the other bed.

Noah stared at the partition. So, it wasn't Julie. He wasn't disappointed, really. He didn't mind being alone. She'd probably become bored and went back to the party.

That was okay. Alone was *his* choice. It was much better than the alternative. He believed that with his whole heart. All he had to do was remember his parents and their marriage. Their fighting and their constant discord.

They'd been so polished in public, because appearance was everything, that no one outside the family would ever have guessed the truth. Noah suspected many marriages were like that—pleasant on the outside, but painful on the inside.

A soft voice broke through his thoughts. "Hey, they said the drugs are helping."

"The pain is better." He opened his eyes to see Julie at his side, looking out of place in her beautiful party dress. "What are you still doing here? I thought you'd want to go looking for excitement."

"I called my friends, and they're taking care of everything at the party. You just close your eyes and relax. I'll stay right here with you." Her hand curled around his. Her gentle touch was sweeter than anything he'd ever known.

He held on tight. "What about your boyfriend?"

"I don't have a boyfriend. I decided you men weren't worth the hassle."

That's right. The broken engagement. "You should be dating someone, a pretty woman like you."

"Me? What about you? A smooth-talker like you has to have five girlfriends on a string. Do you want me to call one of them so she can play your angel of mercy?"

"I'll leave that to you."

"I'm terrible at mercy, but I can teach you the alphabet."

"I already know it."

"How about finger painting? How to color between the lines?"

"Already mastered both." He could picture her, firmly guiding a classroom of small children. Her students probably adored her. "I'm hooked up to all these monitors, but I am cognizant enough to notice you changed the subject."

"Which subject?"

She looked to be all innocence, but she didn't fool him. He hadn't built his company from a basement operation by luck alone. "Your boyfriend. He's probably pining for you, brokenhearted."

"I'm not dating anyone, Mr. Nosy. I think they gave you too many painkillers. If you were in more pain, you wouldn't have the energy to interrogate me."

"It helps pass the time."

"Then maybe I should torture you?" She lifted her chin, all challenge, all sparkle. "I guess I don't have the time. They've come to take you away."

An orderly pulled back the curtain. "They're ready for you down at X ray."

X ray. That didn't sound too painful.

Julie's squeezed his hand before she stepped away, a final show of comfort, and then they were wheeling him away, leaving her behind.

He'd never felt more alone in his life.

Chapter Five

The glow from the church windows seemed to light up the parking lot, reflecting off the falling snow. Noah took another swig from the water bottle he'd picked up at the drugstore. The pain pills were in his breast pocket, unopened. He was hurting, but it was getting better.

It looked as though tomorrow morning he'd be going in for more tests. He'd talked the doctor out of an overnight hospital stay, but a flight back tonight was out. Whatever the problem was, it needed to be dealt with. Noah clamped his jaw tight. He hated doctors.

"Are you sure you can make it home?" Julie pulled the parking brake, leaving the engine idling. "I can drive you. Granddad can return Nora's car tomorrow morning."

What was with Julie? Why was she helping him? Nobody was *that* nice. That was the lesson life always seemed to teach him. Every time he trusted a woman, she turned out to be someone different. Someone who wanted something from him. Every single time.

The glow from the dash lights illuminated the concern on her heart-shaped face. A genuine concern, no different from what she'd shown the little girl they'd rescued in the storm. Julie Renton was a bona fide nice person. There was no other explanation for it.

"You can stop helping me, now." He tugged the tie from his pocket and shook the folds from it. "Because of me, you missed most of the party you planned and paid for. You missed being with your friends. You didn't get dinner or dessert."

"True, but I got a lovely tour of the hospital and a new friend. That's not a bad deal."

"Thanks for hanging out with me." He didn't know quite how to say it. How did you tell someone you hardly knew how alone you were? "You made things better for me."

"You really scared me, Noah."

"I scared me, too." Words caught in his throat. He wasn't used to speaking honestly about his fears.

"I'd better get in there." He grabbed the door handle. Didn't want to go. "About the E.R. visit. You won't say anything to my grandmother?"

"It's yours to tell. Or not."

He leaned across the seat and kissed her cheek.

Her hair smelled as fresh as strawberries. Her sweetness clung to him as he opened the door. "Thank you."

His chest felt tight with emotions. He couldn't begin to sort them out, so he stepped into the cold and dark. The snow was slick beneath his shoes as he circled the truck.

He caught her elbow as she was climbing from the cab, her long skirt swirling in the wind. "Couldn't wait for me to open your door, could you? Whoever the guy was who broke your heart, he was no gentleman."

"So, you've already heard about that? Nothing's a secret in a small town." Snow clung to her hair, shimmering like priceless diamonds in the light, this friend the Lord had sent to him on this night. "No, he wasn't. If he'd been more like you, I might have kept him."

"If he were rich, you mean." Noah wasn't fooled. He knew the way the world worked. Love always had its price.

"No." Julie sounded angry, and she looked angry, too. "If he were as nice as you. Kind beats out rich any day."

She was a kindergarten teacher. He had to remember that. Julie Renton spent her days reading stories to little kids and teaching the alphabet. She probably drew happy faces in the dots over her *i*'s and put gold stars on every child's school page. She wore rose-colored glasses to view the world, but it was a nice outlook. It made him like her more.

"The caterer's truck is still here." Julie pointed through the hazy snow to a white van parked at the edge of the crowded lot. "I'm going to go scare up a couple plates of food. There has to be leftovers."

"See if there's any cake left. Chocolate, if they have it."

"Chocolate, huh? I may be forced to raise my opinion of you."

"Of me? What? Do you think I'm an undesirable city slicker?"

"With those shoes? You betcha. Any self-respecting Montanan wears boots."

"You're in heels."

"True, but I couldn't find a pair of boots to match my dress."

"I had the same problem, so I went with trousers." He held the door, wincing a bit. His chest was still sore, but it hardly mattered. Julie was chuckling at him, and it had been a long while since he'd had anyone to laugh with.

Julie couldn't believe it. Noah was standing up straight. Except for the strain at his jaw and the dark circles beneath his eyes, no one would ever know he was hurting. He moved slowly, holding his grandmother tenderly, making her laugh as they danced to a Cole Porter tune.

She set Noah's plate on the table.

"Julie, what happened?" Misty circled the table. "I've been worried about you. Susan said she thought you were at the hospital. She heard sirens in the background. Are you okay?"

"I'm fine." She'd sworn to keep Noah's secret, so she didn't elaborate. "You're wonderful for managing all this. I owe you and Susan a dinner out, my treat."

"I would hope so." Susan joined them, feigning distress. "It was a nightmare. One disaster after another."

Misty winked. "That's right. Maybe you should spring for lunch *and* dinner."

"Funny." Julie collapsed into the closest chair. "Everything went all right?"

"Perfect. You had everything done ahead of time." Susan dropped into the chair next to her. "You and Mr. Billionaire left about the same time."

"Mysteriously," Misty added. "Is he nice?"

"Very." He had been terribly ill, but he danced the last dance of the night with his grandmother. Without a single word of complaint. That was nice, in her book.

Susan slipped off one high heel and rubbed her toes. "Is it true what everyone's saying? Did he really rescue the little Corey girl?"

"He did." The image of him wading through the harsh storm-tossed creek with little Hailey safe in his arms remained. She'd never forget it. "I saw it with my own two eyes."

"You were alone with him then, too." Susan's gaze narrowed. "Is there something you want to tell us? Did you go steal that handsome rich man right out from under us?"

"I wish." Julie clamped her hand over her mouth. Where had that come from?

"I knew it!" Misty clapped her hands with glee. "Fine, if I have to lose him to someone, it may as well be to my best friend. As long as you let me come stay at your Hawaii beach house."

"Yeah. And at your New York penthouse," Susan chimed in.

"And sail on your multimillion-dollar yacht."

Julie's face flamed. "Enough, you two. Heaven's sake, I played chauffeur for the man. I didn't propose to him."

"Why not?" Susan demanded with a wink.

"I would have." Misty waggled her brows.

"Ladies." A man's pleasant baritone broke through their laughter—Noah. "I couldn't help noticing the beautiful women at this table."

Julie's face burned hotter. How much of their conversation had Noah heard? He stood there, humor curving his mouth, a little too pale and very tired looking. But every bit a gentleman as he took Susan by the elbow and swept her out of her seat.

"Did you see that?" Misty drained all the lemon-lime punch from her glass. "He simply whisked her away. Just like on my favorite soap, when Pierce whisked Jessica away and they fell in love. Oh, this is too unbelievable.''

"Unbelievable.'' There was no other word for it.

"Is he a good dancer?''

"Oh, yeah.'' Julie couldn't help sighing a little as she watched Noah spin Susan around, slow and sweet. She knew exactly what it felt like to be swept away by him.

"Look at your grandfather,'' Misty whispered. "He was pretty worried where you went, but I smoothed things over. Look at the way Nora is gazing into his eyes. Now, *that's* true love.''

Absolutely. Granddad held Nora tenderly, distinguished in his dark jacket and white shirt, joy transforming him. See? True love did exist. She couldn't wish for more for her granddad. *Thank you, Father, for bringing love into his life again.*

"Since I'm not needed here, I'll go help clean up.'' Julie climbed to her feet, stealing one more look in Noah's direction. He had Susan laughing and the attention of every woman in the room.

Misty pushed out of her chair. "I'll give you a hand, too, since Susan has the billionaire all to herself.''

"Stay put. I happen to know you're next.''

"Really? Oh, thank you!''

Several people stopped Julie on the way to the kitchen to ask where she'd been or to comment on the lovely party. It was beautiful. Candles flickered gentle and low. The decorations sparkled like stardust. Flowers scented the air as she pushed open the kitchen door.

"The caterers are almost done." Her friend Karen, who owned the town coffee shop, plunged her hands into the sink. Water sloshed as she scrubbed a pot. "Thought I'd pitch in, so we wouldn't be here cleaning up all night."

"You're an angel." Julie took a dish towel from a nearby shelf and grabbed a soup kettle from the drying rack.

She and Karen talked while they washed and dried. The music from the band kept them entertained, and so did the caterers who dropped nearly everything as they packed their van.

Susan poked her head in after a while. "Harold and Nora are getting ready to leave."

Julie left the dishes and joined the crowd in a long line down the hallway. Shouts of good wishes and congratulations rang in the corridor as Nora and Granddad paraded by. Julie called out her good wishes along with everyone else.

"Hey, beautiful."

"Noah!" She spun around, startled to see him there, looking pallid. "Why are you still here?"

"I'm ready to leave. Just wanted to see them off."

The party was dispersing, voices ringing out in the hallway so loud, it was hard to hear. Julie leaned closer. "This is why you were in the emergency room. I bet you weren't feeling well all day, and you ignored it."

"I refuse to answer that. I'm pleading the Fifth."

For the first time, she got a really good look at Noah Ashton. He wasn't perfect like some airbrushed magazine-cover photograph. Not flawless like a dreamed-up perfect man. He was real and strong and vulnerable all at once, and a man who kept his promises.

That mattered to her. "You didn't have to dance with my friends tonight."

"I wanted to. You see, there's this very nice person who helped me tonight. I didn't want to let her down."

"You do that a lot, I bet. Try not to let people down."

"I try." His gaze strayed to the doorway, where Nora was waving out the passenger window of Harold's pickup.

Noah was so different from the man she expected. Julie touched his sleeve. "I'll be inside if you need anything. Like a ride home. You can't drive if you take painkillers."

"I know." He nodded, in control. "I'm fine."

She watched him take a few steps. "You're limping."

"I'm not." He shuffled forward. "My ankle is tired from all that dancing."

"You're hurting. You should take a pill and let me drive you home."

"My knee's tired, too. I'll just take it slow down the hall. I'm fine."

"You keep saying that."

"Maybe that'll make it true." He tossed her a wink before shouldering through the door.

Julie watched him limp all the way to his grandmother's car.

A handful of kids ran down the hallway, coats dragging, shouting as they went. A cold draft from the open door breezed over her, reminding her that she had work to do. She could still see Noah through the glass in the door, digging car keys from his pocket.

Nice man. Not at all what she'd expected and exactly the kind of man she liked. Didn't that spell trouble?

He'd made it home. Noah took a deep breath, said a prayer of thanks and turned off the engine. Snow pelted the windshield as he sat in the silence. The pain was coming back in slow but steady increments. Probably because the drugs he'd received in the emergency room were wearing off.

Maybe he would take one of the pills from the brown plastic bottle in his jacket pocket. Just to make it through until morning. More tests were awaiting him, starting at 8:00 a.m., when he was supposed to be flying home. There was a finance meeting on Monday morning. He couldn't miss it.

Pain pulsed in the middle of his diaphragm, as if someone was trying to tell him to pay attention.

Okay, maybe he'd keep the doctor's appointment. Then he'd worry about his company.

Moving carefully, he climbed out into the winter weather. The night was bitter cold and dark. Driving snow blew him off course. A lilac bush tried to ambush him on the way to the front porch, but he escaped up the steps.

"Noah, come in." Nanna called the instant he opened the door. "My stars, look at you. You're all alone. I can't believe it. I saw you dancing with so many lovely young ladies, why, I kept hoping you'd find my future granddaughter-in-law."

"Keep dreaming, gorgeous." He leaned stiffly, trying not to wince, to kiss her cheek, and noticed the distinguished gentleman sitting on the couch. "Good evening, Harold. You two look as if you need to be alone. I'll just head upstairs."

"Some awfully pretty girls." Nanna bounded up from the sofa, refusing to be distracted. "And what did you do? You made yourself scarce. A business call came up, and that was more important than dancing with eligible young women."

He couldn't lie to her, but he couldn't tell her about the emergency room. "I was otherwise engaged, it's true, but how can you blame me? After dancing with the loveliest lady in the room, those other women paled by comparison."

"You stop trying to charm me." Nanna blushed, pleasure wreathing her face. "I know I ought to be mad at you, running off the way you did, but dancing with you was such a treat, I'll have to forgive you this once. When will you learn that your work isn't everything? Even our good Lord rested on the seventh day.''

''I've heard that somewhere before.'' He let his grandmother wrap him in a warm hug. She felt so small and fragile, so much love and goodness. Tenderness warmed him, and he wanted to protect her. He'd do anything to make her world right.

Nanna stepped away, leaving the scent of her violet perfume on his jacket. ''It's cold tonight, and if this wind keeps up, we're likely to lose power. I'll run upstairs and fetch a few blankets, just in case.''

''I can do it, Nanna. I'm a big boy.''

''Stuff and nonsense.'' She was already heading toward the stairs. ''You two can get to know each other while I'm gone.''

He did want to get to know Harold Renton, just not right now. Exhaustion weighed him down, and he eyed Mr. Renton warily.

Harold nodded in the way men from the country did, his drawl unassuming. ''Counted on seeing you at the dinner tonight. My granddaughter went to some trouble to seat you at our table. You hurt your grandmother when you didn't show.''

There was no accusation to the man's words. Just hard plain fact. Noah couldn't find fault with that. He had missed dinner. ''I can only apologize.''

''Might be good to consider her feelings for a change. She thinks the sun rises and sets by you.''

"I think the same of her. If you don't know that, then you and I have nothing to say." Pain curled deep in his chest, but Noah didn't back down. This man was a stranger. Maybe good, maybe bad. Noah didn't know for sure. But he'd had a long day, and he wasn't in the mood.

The kitchen was quiet and welcoming, with a light over the sink guiding his way. He filled a cup with water and popped it into the microwave. While the machine hummed, he lifted the lid from the cookie jar and rummaged inside.

What was he going to do about Harold? Noah tugged two cookies from the ceramic beehive cookie jar and replaced the lid. Because of the medical tests, he'd be staying here for at least another day. That gave him plenty of time to find a detective.

That felt kinda sneaky, but how else was he going to protect his grandmother? He'd seen her tonight, alight with love for this Harold guy. She was too trusting. Noah had to take care of her. All that mattered was her welfare.

The microwave beeped, drawing him back to the room. He took a bite out of the cookie—raisin oatmeal—and removed the cup out of the microwave. Steam wafted off the heated water as he went in search of a tea bag.

"I didn't have a chance to buy any more of that fancy tea you like." Nanna tapped into the kitchen. "Some nice chamomile ought to help what ails you."

"I'm fine." It wasn't a lie. He was suffering from stress, like any businessman in his position. That's all the doctors were going to find out come morning—stress. He'd start working out regularly, and he'd be all right. No need to worry his grandmother.

"You can't blame me for fussing over my only grandson." She swept a jar from the counter and dug out a tea bag. "Here, try this. It's not fancy, but it will help you sleep. You look exhausted, Noah. No doubt from that lifestyle of yours."

"Here we go again." He loved his grandmother. That's why he wasn't going to argue with her, so he took the tea bag and dunked it into his cup. "Fine. I'll drink this tea that smells like weeds, to make you happy."

"Wonderful! That's my boy." She squeezed his arm in approval. "I hope you won't be up late on that computer of yours. You need a good night's rest. I'll feel better when I see those dark circles of yours gone for good."

"I like it when a beautiful woman fusses over me." He doused the tea bag a few more times. "That's why I'm not even going to argue with you tonight."

"Wise man." She beamed her approval. "I'd better see your light off when I come up to bed, or they'll be trouble to pay."

"Yes, ma'am."

"And drink every last drop of that tea, you hear?" She cared. It felt good. Noah couldn't disappoint her. "I'll drink every last drop. Even if it tastes as bad as it smells."

"Sleep well, my Noah." She blew him a kiss across the kitchen. When she disappeared down the hall, he stood listening to her steps, missing her.

She'd been his to care for, for as long as he'd been grown up enough to do things for her. Manage her finances and make sure she had everything she desired. He'd watched out for her, flown her out for holidays and vacations. Called her faithfully every week.

And now there was this Harold. This man who was going to be responsible for Nanna. Who wanted to marry her.

Marriage. That single word could cinch up Noah's stomach tighter than anything could. What if Harold didn't treat Nanna right? What if he hurt her? Ran off with her money, or broke her dreams right along with her heart?

In Noah's view, those outcomes were more probable than the happily-ever-after other people imagined.

Noah's guts burned. Pain pounded in his chest. This had to be upsetting him more than he realized.

Taking the weed tea and the remaining cookie, he climbed the steps to the cooler second story. Boards squeaked beneath his shoes. A dim light lit his way to the top.

One thing for sure, this house needed a remodel. Nanna could trip and fall on these stairs. And what about that draft? She could catch pneumonia, and at her age that was a concern.

He'd talk to her about it at breakfast. But for now, he'd check his messages and his e-mail. Make sure no crisis was brewing back home.

The door whispered on old hinges in the guest room at the end of the hall. Lamplight glowed from the night table near an old fashioned, four-poster bed. Several of Nanna's afghans were folded at the foot of the bed, topped by her page-worn Bible. A yellow ribbon marked one of the pages.

Leave it to Nanna to speak to him, even when she wasn't in the room. Noah set aside the tea and cookie and opened the precious book. Nanna had chosen a passage from Psalms. "Lord, remind me how brief my time on earth will be. Remind me that my days are numbered, and that my life is fleeing away."

He sat down on the bed. Okay, he could see where she was going with this. He kept reading. "We are merely moving shadows, and all our busy rushing ends in nothing."

Like an arrow hitting its target, Noah felt the words take root in his heart. Fine, he knew he was unhappy. Stress was taking a toll. He had an appointment in the morning for blood tests, a CT scan and an MRI. Pain roared like a jackhammer in his chest.

He took the bottle of pills from his jacket pocket and studied them. There were only a few, enough to get him through until morning. He wasn't going to take one. He knew, as had happened last time, the pain was winding down. By morning, he'd feel okay. Not great, but not horrible, either.

"We need more tests." That's what the doctor had told him when Julie had gone to find a pay phone. "We could be looking at a real problem."

Help me, Lord. Noah bowed his head and prayed.

Chapter Six

Julie yawned, refusing to think about how late she'd been out last night. She was no night owl, and she was paying for it this morning. Her alarm clock had rousted her from sleep hours ago, and she was still in the sweats she'd pulled on over her nightshirt.

Caffeine was bound to help. She took a sip from her steaming cup of coffee and flipped open the book in front of her. Were they making the print smaller today? No, her eyes were tired. The cleanup had gone later than she'd planned, but that wasn't the real reason she was tired. She'd tossed and turned half the night.

She'd been worried about Noah Ashton. He'd been in so much pain. She'd been afraid for him, and she still was.

Maybe she ought to call, after all. It was a few

minutes past nine. Surely Nora had been up for hours. With any luck, Noah was back from his early-morning appointment.

A knock at the door echoed through the house. Julie leaned in her chair to get a good view out the door. There was a green pickup visible through the glass door. Granddad! What was he doing here?

Probably come to plow her driveway. She turned the dead bolt and yanked open the door. "Perfect timing. The coffee just finished brewing."

"I'll take you up on that offer." Granddad knocked the snow off his boots on the small deck before venturing inside. "Whew, it's cold out there. We've got a good ten inches out there, and it's still falling. Thought I'd warm up before I clear your driveway."

"Want some muffins?" Julie snatched a ceramic mug from the cupboard and reached for the glass carafe.

"Don't go to any trouble for me." He went straight to the pink baker's box on the corner of her kitchen island. "That was some party. You did a good job, girl. Sure made my Nora happy."

"I think you make her happy." Julie filled the cup with steaming coffee. "You want sugar with this?"

"Takin' it black today." Granddad kicked out a chair and plopped into it. "That's a nice flower you got there."

"What flower?" Julie turned from the counter.

"That one, right there."

There, in the center of the table, right next to her devotional, was Noah's corsage. The single white rose looked as perfect as ever.

"It's nothing." She gave Granddad his coffee and snatched the flower from its place on her table. "And since it's nothing and means nothing at all, I'm going to go put this in the fridge."

"Are you gonna fess up? Tell me who bought it for you?"

"It's top secret. Classified by the government and everything."

"You're fibbing, girl, and that tells me what I need to know." Granddad looked proud of himself. "Who's your new beau?"

"Nosy, aren't you?"

"Just looking out for my granddaughter. It's a grandfather's job."

"Well, it's a granddaughter's job to keep you guessing." Julie grabbed a plate from the shelf and carried it to the table. "There is no boyfriend. You know why."

"You just need time to find the right one, that's all." Granddad unwrapped his blueberry muffin. "Look at me, getting married at this time in my life. Figured I'd be alone for the rest of my days, and the Good Lord saw fit to send Nora my way. Only He knows what's in store for you."

"I think God has already told me that." The empty place on her left ring finger still remained both a memory and a humiliation. Only Granddad knew how much. Determined to change the subject, Julie slid the plate in front of him. "I noticed your lights were on late when I drove by last night. What were you doing up?"

Granddad reached for the butter dish. "Couldn't get to sleep. Guess the party had me all charged up."

"You don't look happy when you say that." Julie pushed a clean knife across the table for him. It was there in the crinkle of his brow and the exhaustion dark beneath his eyes. Something was making him unhappy. "What happened?"

"Nora and I had a little disagreement." Granddad dropped the muffin on his plate and left it there. He sighed, looking miserable.

Julie wanted to comfort him, to reassure him that everything would be all right, and that he and Nora would work out their problems. But she'd been in this same place, and it hadn't turned out okay. Wedding plans were easy enough to cancel, but the cost to the heart was staggering.

"I'm sorry." It was all she could say. "Is there anything I can do?"

"Yep. Help that grandson of hers pack up and get the blazes out of here." Granddad rubbed his brow. "Pardon me for sayin' that. I get my back up when I talk about that young man."

"What happened?"

"I just spoke my mind. Should've thought about it first, but I figured it needed to be said. It wasn't right the way he left the party like that. He's always off doing what he wants to do. Nora won't admit it, but it hurt her when he left. I can't stand her hurting. I told him about it, but he didn't apologize. Just told me I didn't know a thing.''

Julie bit her bottom lip. So, Noah had decided to keep his condition secret. What should she say now? She'd given her word to him. She couldn't break it, but she couldn't stand to see her grandfather hurting. ''I think Noah had a good reason to leave, and he *did* return to the dance.''

''She forgives him for anything.''

''That reminds me of another grandparent I know. Let me think who it would be....''

''Not me.'' Granddad blushed a little, relaxing as he reached for the coffee mug. ''That's different. I don't indulge you. I don't look the other way or make excuses. You're a good, responsible girl, nothing at all like...'' Granddad sighed. ''No, I've vowed not to say an unkind word. I shouldn't be making judgments, but if he makes Nora sad one more time...''

''The trouble is when you really love someone, you hurt for them, too.'' Julie knew something about that. ''I know how you feel. You want to protect Nora. That's wonderful. But you don't know what happened last night.''

''And you do? I noticed you were missing. Your friends made a few excuses, how you'd just ran out on an errand and whatnot. Don't think I didn't notice how you left about the same time he did. And came back, too.''

"You can say his name, Granddad. Noah's different from what I expected. You should get to know him.''

"When? He's probably halfway to New York by now.''

Julie glanced at the clock. Noah's pain was so severe, what if there was something terribly wrong? No one else knew where he was or what he was going through. "I like Noah, Granddad. You might, too, if you gave him half a chance.''

"I don't need advice from you, missy.'' He winked, to soften the impact of his words. "What I need is to finish this coffee so I can get back to work. He gave you that flower, did he?''

"If he did, that would make him a nice guy. Mean guys don't go around giving corsages to women they don't know.''

"He got one for Nora, too. Giving her flowers is *my* job.''

Mystery solved. Julie reached across the table for her grandfather's muffin. "Noah's been looking after his grandmother for a long time. It's probably going to be hard for him to step aside and let someone else take over. Even someone as wonderful as you.''

"You're takin' his side.''

"No way. I'm firmly on yours.'' She grabbed the knife and buttered the muffin. "You can't let anything stand in the way of your special love for your bride. It's that simple. Noah adores his grand-mother.''

"Adores her, or her money?''

"Granddad!''

He looked fierce and protective and every bit a hard, seasoned cowboy. He looked ready for a fight. Her gentle granddad! He fisted his hands. "He's the one who takes care of her finances. Nora has no idea of her net worth. She has to call him to transfer money if she needs it. He's generous and says he takes care of her, but who knows if he's taking advantage of her.''

"Noah wouldn't do that.'' She was certain of it. The man who'd risked his life in an electrical storm and crossed a flooding creek to save a child, had to have a good heart. A man who'd suffer pain and fear alone, so he wouldn't worry his grandmother, had to be protecting her, not out to hurt her. "Noah wouldn't, Granddad. Trust me.''

"I'd sure like to, but the truth is, you don't know Noah Ashton any more than I do. Thought I could get to know him last night. Talk to him a bit, but then he ran off.''

"He had a good reason. He wouldn't travel all the way from New York just to stand up his grand-mother.''

Granddad's fists relaxed. "Maybe you're right, and maybe that grandson of hers is overprotective.''

"No one I know is like that.''

Granddad blushed a little, taking a bite of muffin.

"Didn't come here to hear the truth. Would've rather gotten some sympathy for my wounded pride. Not told I was wrong."

"You're not wrong. You're in love." Julie pushed the sugar bowl across the table. "Forget plowing the driveway. I'll take care of it. You go find Nora and apologize."

"Maybe I can use your phone. Give her a call or something."

"You know where it is."

Julie flipped open her devotional as he left the room. She wanted happiness for him, more than anything. This would work itself out. Noah was a good man, and he hadn't come here to interfere. He'd given his word.

In the living room, at the far side of the house, she heard Granddad's rumbling voice as he spoke to his fiancée. The furnace kicked on, breezing warm air across her slippered feet. The cat, curled in his cat bed next to the vent, stretched and yawned, content. The storm outside buffeted the windows but couldn't touch him.

Julie turned her attention to the opened page in her devotional. "As a face is reflected in water, so the heart reflects the man."

She thought of Noah. Maybe, she'd give him a call. Find out if he was back from his appointment, see if he needed a friend.

Tough morning. Noah spotted the neon window sign that read Espresso in blue lettering and pulled off the main road through town. There wasn't any traffic so he didn't need to wait. Snow crunched beneath the tires as he slid to a slow stop against the curb.

His hands were still shaking. The doctor will be in touch, they'd said. What did that mean? Good news? Bad news? Either way, he was forced to wait for it.

How was he going to go home to Nanna like this? She'd see through him this time, for sure. Two weeks ago, he'd been able to write this off as a bad case of stress and too many chili peppers in his enchilada. He couldn't make excuses today. The visit to the doctor was as real as it got. They'd taken blood tests to detect invasive cancer.

Please don't let it be that. Noah rubbed at the sudden pain behind his temple. It was too much to think about. He wasn't going to do it, tear himself up inside worrying over what was out of his control.

No, he was going to be proactive. Go about his life as usual until he heard from the doctor. He'd stay in Montana at least another day. Maybe spend time with his grandmother, or give his sister a call…

That wouldn't work. Nanna and Hope would take one look at him and know something was wrong. He took a deep breath and let it out slowly, trying to figure out what to do. He could get ahold of Julie and see what she was up to today. She'd been great to him last night. He owed her. Big-time.

* * *

Thank goodness he'd gotten ahold of her. He'd buy her a cup of coffee and thank her again. It was the least he could do.

Taking it easy, he climbed out of the car. This small piece of Montana seemed like another world. Right here, in the middle of town, silence met his ears. Peace filtered around him. The air smelled fresh and crisp, like something wonderful that could never be bottled or packaged. Snow shifted over him as he locked the car door.

"Hey, city slicker." Julie Renton tromped through the snowy street without even looking for traffic. Her hiking boots kept her from slipping as she headed his way. "Around here nobody locks their doors."

"Guess I'm not blending in." He tucked the keys into his wool trousers. "I didn't have time to hit the Western store and buy a Stetson and jeans."

"And boots."

"Are you ready for some coffee?"

She tossed the fringed end of her scarf over her shoulder. "Are you kidding? I'm always ready for coffee."

"My kind of girl." Noah headed for the shoveled sidewalk.

"So, are you going to tell me what happened this morning?" Julie led the way up the sidewalk, where the coffee shop gleamed like a beacon of light and modern heating. "What did the doctor say?"

"Since it's Saturday, he'll have to get back to

me." Saying it that way didn't sound scary at all. He could be awaiting the results of a sore throat or a rapidly growing wart. It didn't have to be anything as grave as cancer. "They told me he'd get back to me by Monday."

"Monday? That's too long to wait. I saw you last night, Noah. I can't believe they let you walk out of Emergency."

"I'm a persuasive man when I want to be."

"I bet you can be, Mr. Billionaire."

"The way you say that sounds as if you don't like billionaires."

"I can't be that judgmental—it goes against my faith. You are the only billionaire I've ever met, and all I can say, is *frightening*."

"I'm that bad?"

"Absolutely."

He grabbed the door for her, the bell tinkling merrily as she swept past him.

She smelled of strawberries and vanilla and snow—awesome and sweet. With the faint scent of strawberries lingering on his coat, he followed her into the shop.

"You're nice to your grandmother, kind to strangers and you're buying me a latte. What's not to like?"

"I'm buying you a latte? I thought you were buying."

"No, no. I'm sure you said you were paying." She was laughing as she reached in her coat pocket. She sauntered up to the counter and called to the young woman behind the counter. "Michelle, I'll have a special, please."

A little white eraser board was propped up behind the cash register. Apple Pie Latte, $2.00, it said in curly handwriting. "Sounds good," he added. "Make it two."

Julie unsnapped her wallet.

He tugged a bill from his pocket and laid it on the counter. "My treat. I mean it. You've done enough for me. It's time I started doing something for you."

"We're even, Noah." Her hand brushed his forearm with the gentlest of touches. "Let's find a table."

He dropped another bill in the tip jar as Julie wove through the nearly empty room, calling out a hello to a group of women in the corner.

What would it be like to know everyone in the coffee shop by name? It was an alien concept.

Julie chose a table along the long wall of windows. "How about this?"

"Looks good." He could see the main street, cloaked in peaceful snow. Couldn't be more than four blocks to the town. It looked like something out of a Western movie. "What do you people do here? There's no sports arena. No museums—"

"Hey, we have the historical museum directly across the street. Except it's closed today."

"I must have missed seeing the sign on the way in to town."

"It happens." Julie shrugged out of her coat. "For your information, buster, there are a lot of things to do here. Wonderful, exciting things you can't find in your basic major city."

"And that would be…"

She rose to the challenge, all fire and life. "Aside from our historical museum, you mean? Well, there is every winter sport you can think of."

"The luge? Bobsled? Curling?"

She gave him her schoolteacher look. "I expect you to behave, Mr. Ashton, and stop thinking you're so smart. I'm talking about cross-country skiing. Downhill skiing. Snowshoeing. Snowmobiling. There's the weekend high school basketball game, but it was away this week."

"You're living the high life, Julie." Noah slung his coat over the back of his chair. "I'm not sure I can keep up with you."

"Is that a challenge?" She lifted her chin, as if she wasn't afraid of him. Not one bit.

"Sure. Exactly what are you challenging me to? A wild walk down Main Street?"

Her schoolteacher look darkened. "I think you definitely need to be taught a lesson, Mr. Ashton. Do you ski at all?"

"Downhill, but I haven't been in years. I never have the time to fly to Colorado for the weekend."

"Well, I'm one up on you. I don't have to fly anywhere for the best skiing I've ever found."

He couldn't resist asking. "Have you ever been out of Montana?"

"Once, when I went to Yellowstone Park, which is about a hundred miles south of here. It's in Wyoming." Her eyes sparkled at him, full of mirth and humor and real friendship.

That was something he didn't get often. "The best skiing, huh? I'm there."

"Great. I'll take you home with me. You can borrow Granddad's skis. You two are about the same height."

"You live with your grandfather?"

"Near him." Julie turned to talk to the waitress who brought their coffee in tall white paper cups.

"Thanks for the great tip, Mr. Ashton." The waitress was probably just out of college. She looked so young.

His ten-year college reunion had been a few summers ago. Over a dozen years had passed since he was that age. Where had the time gone? Noah didn't know. His life had become a blur of work, meetings and loneliness.

It felt pretty great sitting here with Julie. She chatted with the waitress a few minutes. He didn't notice what she was saying. Only the friendly way she treated everyone. It was the same way she treated him, and he liked it.

Noah popped the top off the cup and tossed the slim red straws onto a napkin. He drank from the brim. The sweet, apple-and-cinnamon-flavored coffee was different. He always ordered his latte without flavoring. Change was nice, he decided. Different, but nice.

"Okay, your time off for good behavior is up." They were alone, and Julie swirled the plastic straws around in her drink. "Confess."

"Maybe I don't want to."

"Then I'll have to torture it out of you." She looked angelic in a soft cable-knit sweater. Her dark hair was drawn back into a bouncy ponytail, leaving airy wisps to frame her heart-shaped face. "Don't smirk at me like that. I'm tough enough to get the truth out of you, mister."

"I'm sure you are." Noah tried not to laugh. She was a pushover—anyone could see that—and in the nicest way. He liked that about her, too. "I'm not smirking. I'm trembling with fear. Don't torture me. I'll tell you anything you want to know."

"I thought so. When my kids misbehave, they have to put their heads down on their desks until I say they can get up."

"Brutal. I wouldn't want that happening to me." Noah winked at her, more charming than any man had the right to be. Then his cell phone rang and he reached into his coat pocket for the phone. "Wait— it's not the doctor. I'll let the voice mail get it."

"They didn't give you any hint about what was going on?"

He shook his head. Dark shocks of hair tumbled over his brow as he leaned forward to tuck the small phone into his coat pocket. "They didn't say anything, and I'm a pretty persuasive guy."

Julie could hear the low, quiet tone of fear in his voice. The humor on his face had drained away, leaving lines around his eyes and mouth, and showing how pale he was. "Are you still in pain?"

"Not much. It's down to a low throb. I keep telling myself it's just an attack of some kind. Like heartburn or something, but..." He shrugged, falling silent. What he didn't say rang loud and clear between them.

He was afraid. She understood. "If you need anything, ask."

"I appreciate that." He swirled the foam around in his cup. "Do you know what I need?"

"I'm clueless. What?"

"To get my mind off this." He squared his wide shoulders. "Want to teach me how to cross-country ski?"

"It's going to cost you. Big."

"How big?"

"Huge. Enormous. I'm a teacher, sure, but right now I'm off-hours. I don't just teach anyone anything for free."

"How about another cup of coffee to go?"

"You're on." Julie reached for her coat. "But first, prepare yourself. You're in for the time of your life."

Chapter Seven

Julie wasn't kidding. Noah stopped at a turnout on the path between tall, snow-bound firs. His breath rose in great clouds in the cold air as he trekked close to the edge.

Wow. Those were some of the best views he'd ever seen. Mountain peaks close enough to touch rose straight up into the clouds. Snow fell in a misty curtain from sky to valley floor, far below, draping endless stands of trees. He breathed in the cold air and felt peace.

Out here, there were no demands. No deadlines. No pressure. Nothing. Just God's beauty.

Julie glided up next to him, stopping expertly with a slight turn. "How are you holding up?"

"Great." Better than great. "I know this pain attack I had is just stress. I get away from my problems for an hour, and every bit of pain is gone.''

''I'm glad.'' Julie knocked snow off her cap. ''Can I make a suggestion? Get rid of your stress.''

''I'll take that under consideration.'' He couldn't get enough of this view. Of this peace shifting over him like the snow. Or maybe it was because of Julie. He couldn't tell. He only knew that he felt as light as the snow tumbling from the sky when she smiled at him.

''Are you ready to go? Or do you need more rest, city boy?''

''This city boy can beat you any day of the week.'' Noah wasn't sure about that, but he liked the way challenge gleamed in Julie's eyes as she tugged her cap lower over her ears.

''You're on. I'll race you over to that meadow down there. See? The one *waaay* down there?'' She pointed with her mittened hand, leaning close.

His chest tightened, quick and hard, like a punch to his midsection. For a split second he thought the pain was coming back, faster than before. But it wasn't pain. It was something else.

''Come on. I'll give you a head start.'' Julie trudged back to the trail, leading the way. Pine boughs rocked, heavy with snow, in her wake and knocked against him.

''I'm such a fantastic skier, *you're* the one who's going to need a head start.'' He winked, and she laughed.

"Right. Fine. We start together, but you're going to be sorry, Mr. Billionaire. C'mon. Line up." She motioned him close, digging in at an imaginary starting line. "Ready?"

"Ready." He dug in beside her.

And they were off at the same moment, shoulder to shoulder. The silence shattered as they crashed along the tree-lined path, knocking limbs. Snow tumbled to the ground. Noah tried to cut over, but he couldn't. Julie was right there, arm braced to keep him right where she wanted him.

She was pulling ahead! "You come back here." He caught her by the back of the jacket and stopped her just enough to take the lead.

"Cheater!" She was laughing.

A snowball pelted him in the middle of the back. "Good aim."

"That was a warm-up, so watch out." She was behind him, skiing hard. One pole was tucked under her arm because there was another snowball in her hand.

He recognized the look in her eye. Okay, he hadn't grabbed her to cheat. He just wanted to grab her. Now he was going to pay for it. "I'm in trouble."

"You bet your bootstraps, buster." She took aim like a major-league pitcher with the bases loaded. Total concentration. Complete confidence.

There was nothing he could do but take the hit like a man. The snowball caught him square in the back of the knee. He went down in an instant, skis flying into the trees, rolling in the snow. He didn't mind the cold creeping down the back of his collar as he climbed onto his feet.

Julie dug in and stopped. "Cheaters never prosper."

"I wasn't cheating." The snow gathered naturally in the palm of his hand. As if it was meant to be. It sailed in a perfect arch, as if he were meant to throw that snowball at this exact moment in time. At this one woman.

The snow broke apart in midair, showering her before impact. Icy crystals rained over her head and knocked her cap off to the side.

"You want trouble? You just got it." She tossed her poles and filled her gloves with snow.

He was on his feet, but it wasn't fast enough. Cold powder hit him square in the face.

"Oops. I didn't mean—" She shrieked as he took off after her.

She was quick, but he was faster. He tackled her from behind, bringing her down in the soft snow. Powder flew as they hit. Her skis shot into the trees as they rolled to a stop.

She landed beside him, laughing. "No fair. You can't tackle me to keep me from winning. Just because you were clumsy and fell down—"

"Clumsy, huh?" He didn't feel like teasing her back. His heart was thundering, he was breathing hard, exhilarated from the cold and the exercise. He reached out and brushed snow from her face with his thumb.

Warmth filled him. Tenderness burned in his chest so hard it almost hurt. It was great being here with her. Having fun. Letting go of his troubles and his responsibilities. And it was because of Julie. He felt real with her. He felt as though she saw the real Noah, when no one else did.

"I'm glad we're friends." He meant it. Down deep. Because he felt a connection to her, he stroked his hand over the curve of her face.

"Me, too." He couldn't interpret the gleam of emotion in her eyes. She climbed to her feet and brushed at the snow caked to her jacket. "As my friend, you'll help me find my skis. Right?"

"Don't be too sure about that." Because one of her skis wasn't that far away from him, he snagged it before she could circle around him. "We're still racing. I intend to win."

"What are you going to do? Hold my ski hostage?"

"Knowing you, it wouldn't stop you. You can probably take this hill on one ski." He handed the thing to her, as he'd planned to do all along.

It was incredible, this way he felt inside. And the scenery... The wind ebbed away, leaving silence in its wake. It was like finding a corner of heaven, new and beautiful and untouched. So far from every unhappiness he felt in his life. So close to the nicest woman he'd ever known.

Noah believed that everything happened for God's reason. The Lord had given him this day, so what was He trying to say?

Noah thought that maybe he already knew.

He caught Julie before she could climb into the thick stand of trees to retrieve her other ski. "Let me. I have a way with firs."

"Those are pines."

He liked that she didn't have a problem putting him in his place. "Fine. I have a way with trees. Stand aside."

Snow-laden boughs slapped him in the face and beat him in the arm as he climbed deeper into the forest. But seizing the lone ski made it all worthwhile. Even more rewarding was the feel of Julie's touch on his arm. It was a real connection. She was a real friend.

He hadn't had one of those in a long time.

He found his skis while Julie waited, and then they were off together, battling it down the mountainside. The wind buffeted him and the cold stung his eyes. It was like flying, wild and fast and thrilling. He fought hard, but at the bottom of the steep hill, Julie inched ahead of him for the win.

Losing had never felt better.

As they skied back to the road, through the forest that edged her property, Julie could still feel the brush of Noah's thumb on her cheek and the touch of his glove to her face. The cold air may have numbed her skin, but that didn't seem to matter. She tried to think of a dozen different things. That didn't help, either. She could remember the look in his eyes. *I'm glad we're friends,* he'd said.

Friends. Yep, that's what they were. Friends. She wouldn't deny it. Didn't expect anything else. But why did men always have to emphasize it, as if she wasn't good enough or attractive enough or special enough to be anything else?

She'd been around the romantic block too many times to mistake friendship for romance. So why were her feelings hurt? Why was she yearning for tenderness from him? It made no sense. It wasn't as if Noah was going to fall for her. He was a billion-aire. She was a small-town girl. A few hours of rec-reation did not make a romance.

Still, disappointment washed over her when she glided across a knoll and the road came into view. Their excursion was over.

He puffed, a little out of breath. "You're slowing down."

So she was. It had been a fun day, and she hated to have it end. The sun was beginning to sink into the western mountains. "Every time I'm out here, I'm never ready for it to end."

Yep, that was it. She just loved skiing so much. It had nothing to do with Noah.

"You were right. This is the best skiing I've ever found." Noah tossed her that grin of his, the one that could make a woman forget every word she'd ever learned. "I can't remember when I've had a better day."

"If that's true, you need to get out more."

"What do you mean *if?* This is pretty special, what you have here. It's amazing. If I want to ski, I have to fly there first."

Julie rolled her eyes. "I hate it when I have to fuel up the Learjet just to go skiing."

"There you go, teasing me again. I don't deserve it."

"That's one theory." She glided around their vehicles parked in her driveway and kept going.

"Just because I have my own jet, doesn't mean I'm a bad guy." He followed her. "Hey, where are you going?"

"That's my house." She took the snow-covered driveway at a fast pace, the wind whistling past her ears.

"*Your* house? Not your grandfather's?"

"I know what you're thinking." She wedge-turned onto the front lawn and circled the house. "How can a kindergarten teacher afford this on her salary?"

"Something like that." It was a little different skiing right through her yard as if it were a trail, but the snow was thick and perfect, leading them to her wood deck in the back.

Julie knelt to release her bindings, and her dark ponytail brushed over her shoulder to touch her face. Her skin was pink from the cold, and Noah had never seen a woman so beautiful. His chest tightened in that strange way again, and he felt…

He didn't know how he felt. He only knew that he liked her.

She straightened, hauling her skis up the steps and leaning them against the side of her house. "A few years ago, Granddad gifted land to each of his grandkids and built us each a house of our choice. This cabin and the eighty acres we just skied on are mine."

"He did what?" Noah leaned the borrowed skis next to Julie's. "He gifted this to you?"

"I know. Pretty great, isn't he?" There was no mistaking the affection in her voice. "He wanted to give us all a better start in life than he had. His ranch is just up the road. You probably saw the house when you drove out here."

Noah hadn't noticed. He was too busy looking around at the incredible view. What she called a cabin was really a two-story log house. Not extravagant, but nice. Very nice. And the land, why, it had to be seriously valuable. Something a man just didn't give away…. "I see where you're going with this. You must have heard Harold and I didn't exactly become best friends."

"I did hear a version of that." She opened one of the glass doors—no keys, she must have left it unlocked—and stomped the snow off her boots. "You could keep an open mind the next time you meet him. Give him half a chance."

"Yeah, yeah. If I wanted a lecture, I could have let Nanna do it." With a wink, he followed Julie inside.

"I'm not lecturing, and *you* asked about the house. What do you think?" She held her arms wide, gesturing to the home she was obviously proud of.

"What's not to like?" He took in the golden honey floors and walls. The open beam ceilings that made the kitchen and eating nook feel spacious. Glass windows stretched from floor to ceiling, showcasing the perfect view of shrouded forest and mountains. "I wouldn't mind looking out at this every day when I come home from work."

"It's great stress reduction. I put up my feet, look out the window and every trouble melts away." She put cups of water in the microwave. "Want to try it? The recliner in the living room is to die for. Once you get in it, it will take an act of Congress to get you out."

In the living room, a gray striped cat took one look at him and raced up the stairs in a blur. He should have figured Julie for a pet person. A blanket was folded on the couch cushion, with telltale cat hair on it. It wasn't too hard to imagine her curled up on the couch watching television at night, with the cat at her side.

It was a pretty big place for one person. He could see his reflection in the living room windows as the sun peeked out, streaking through the glass. The view was even better from here. A man who'd given this to his granddaughter probably wasn't short on cash.

"How many grandkids are there?"

"Ten of us." Julie sounded pleased with herself.

She ought to be. He'd been determined to find out Harold's true motives. True love was possible, but there were other more likely reasons.

Greed. He saw every day what people would do for the almighty dollar, as if that was what truly mattered. Women he'd dated and he'd thought he'd been in love with. Friends that wound up betraying him. Even his family. Whenever Mom or Dad gave him a call, as rare as that was, it was because they needed a few hundred grand to get them by.

"I hope you like hot chocolate with lots of marshmallows." Julie breezed into the room in her stocking feet, the hem of her jeans wet with snow. She carried two brimming mugs and thrust one at him. "You don't look like a marshmallow kind of guy, but too bad. You're getting them anyway."

"What does that mean? I am a marshmallow kind of guy." The cup was hot against his fingers, the chocolate aroma rich and sweet. The marshmallows melted into a foamy froth. "As sweet as can be."

"Do I look gullible?" She grabbed a remote and pressed a button. The fireplace in the corner roared to life. "You're a self-made man, according to all my friends who read that recent magazine article about you."

"I inherited my first million, but made the rest

myself.'' He took the recliner. ''That doesn't make me ruthless. Maybe I made my fortune by accident.''

''By accident? How do you do that, I'd like to know. I love teaching—don't get me wrong—but I wouldn't mind being accidentally wealthy.'' She sat on the edge of the wide coffee table, chin up, all challenge.

She didn't believe him when he'd said his success was an accident. Fine. She would.

''This is something you won't read in any magazine. I never admit this to anyone else. Probably because then I'd look like an incompetent who shouldn't be in charge of a company.''

''Ooh, now I'm curious.'' She leaned forward, and he felt as if he could tell her anything.

''I was fresh out of business school with my MBA in hand. The last thing I wanted to do was work with my father. He has a consulting firm and he was pressuring me to join him. But I'd come into my money that summer, so I rented office space in the basement of this old building in Queens. I set up shop and wrote code with a buddy of mine. By Christmas, we had a financial software package on the market, for trading stocks electronically. By spring, I quadrupled my inheritance.''

''I thought you ran this huge electronics conglomerate.''

''It started out as a small software venture. I was just doing what I loved to do. It snowballed. No, it exploded like a ton of dynamite and buried my life.''

He felt a sense of loss he couldn't explain and didn't know where it came from. "So I made billions and built a huge company, and I never intended to do it."

He took a sip of hot chocolate, and the sweetness soothed that unsettled feeling in his stomach. "Julie, promise me something. Don't tell the stockholders I admitted that."

"Cross my heart." She said it like a promise she would keep for the rest of her days.

She was too good to be true, and he was thankful she was his friend.

She took a sip of hot chocolate. Marshmallow clung to her upper lip. The tip of her tongue swiped the sweetness away.

Before he knew what he was doing, he reached across the distance between them. Her lips felt like warmed satin against his fingertip. "You missed a spot."

"I bet the women you spend time with don't spill marshmallow fluff all over themselves."

"No, they don't." His fingers stroked the corner of her mouth. His touch felt tender and amazing.

She sparkled all the way down to her toes. No man had ever made her feel like this.

He withdrew, but he didn't ease back into the chair. He placed his elbows on his knees, remaining close. So close she could see the black flecks in his dark eyes. It would take nothing at all for him to lean forward and kiss her. She almost wanted him to.

Romantic doom, remember? It was hard, but she managed to slide away from him without spilling her hot chocolate or letting her feelings show.

The microwave dinged, saving her. Instead of running away from being so close to him, it looked as if she were leaving for completely valid reasons.

Noah seemed unaware as he straightened, stood up and paced to the far window. The sunlight was waning, the world outside somber and brooding.

Friends, he had said wisely, and she wholeheartedly agreed. A man like Noah Ashton was wrong for her.

The chili was steaming, and she gave it a good stir.

"Smells good." Noah wandered into the kitchen, stretching. "Homemade?"

"The only kind." She slipped a plate piled with cornbread slices into the microwave and hit the start button. "What do you want to drink? I have vanilla soda or root beer."

"You pick." He sidled past her to the sink and turned on the faucet. The scent of berries filled the air as he pumped out a few dollops of soft soap.

There was a jingling sound, but it wasn't the microwave.

"My cell." Noah's hands were in the water. "It's in my coat. Can you grab it?"

It could be the doctor. She could feel his urgency. She dashed to the table, where his jacket was hanging over the back of a chair, and found the phone by feel.

"If it's from area code 212, let the voice mail get it." He turned off the faucet. "I can always get back—"

Kline Detective Agency, it said on the caller ID screen. Julie stared at it for a moment, and the ringing stopped.

"Is it the doctor?" Noah was dripping water on the floor. He grabbed the phone with his wet hands, worry harsh on his face as he read the screen.

Julie turned away. It was none of her business who was calling Noah. It could be a wrong number. It could be anything.

Then why was he so quiet?

"I'll return that call later." He tucked the phone back into his coat pocket.

"Sure." She carried the bowls to the table. She wasn't going to make any judgments or any conclusions. The pit of her stomach felt oddly empty. Noah wouldn't have Granddad investigated, right? That was something people only did on television.

Noah punched open the microwave door and brought the cornbread to the table for her.

The silence in the kitchen felt enormous. He could hear every footstep. The scrape of wood against the tile floor seemed so loud. Or maybe it was his guilty conscience.

He shouldn't have asked Julie to catch the phone. He didn't think the detective would get back to him so fast. The doctor was supposed to be the one calling, and no way had Noah wanted to hear bad news on his voice mail.

Now, he regretted his impatience. Julie was very quiet as she set spoons and knives on the table. She pushed aside a neat pile of construction paper. Looked as if she'd been cutting out big block letters for a classroom bulletin board.

She waited until she was seated to say grace. He muttered "Amen," and reached for the paper napkin.

She looked upset, and he was a smart enough man to steer clear of the phone call topic. So he said what was on his mind. "What do you think of marriage?"

Her spoon hit the bowl with a clatter. "Do you mean the upcoming wedding or are you talking about marriage in general?"

Uh-oh. She sounded really angry. He started backpedaling. "Marriage in general. It sounds like your parents divorced, too."

"I didn't know that was any of your business." She said it nicely, but there was no mistaking the way she glared at him.

Yep, she was mad. He wasn't going to get out of this unscathed. He may as well face up to it. "I didn't mean for you to know about the detective."

"Why should I? You aren't investigating my grandfather, right?" She folded her hands neatly on the table in front of her. "That detective was calling about something else, right?"

"No." He felt really bad, so he took a bite of chili.

He was amazingly hungry. "After being with you today, I decided I didn't need a P.I."

"So, you thought you had the right to investigate him?"

It was perfectly legal, he wanted to point out, but he decided to take the diplomatic course. Because he really did feel guilty. "I made a mistake. I'll pay the detective what I owe him, but I won't ask for the information."

"I see. That makes it all right?"

"No." He didn't want to hurt her. "I'm sorry. My grandmother is a very wealthy woman, and I have the right to protect her."

"You've come to stop the wedding, haven't you? You're just not going to admit it."

"I admit it. I don't think marriage is a good idea in general, but Harold seems to make Nanna happier than I've ever seen her. Ever. That's worth something."

She pushed away from the table. How could she have been so wrong about Noah? "You took one look at my grandfather and thought, 'Now there's someone to suspect.' Look at the way he helps his grandchildren and attends church on Sunday and donates his time at Young Life. It's all a front. He's really a romancer of rich women."

"Julie." Noah stood, and looked pained, his hands held out as if he wasn't sure he should touch her or defend himself from her. "It wasn't like that. Really. Could you let me apologize?"

"Apologize? That won't change anything." She couldn't believe she'd been so gullible. She'd been taken in by Noah, too. She'd *trusted* him, and he'd been using her! "You spent the day with me to gather information on my grandfather."

"No! That's not true."

"How can I believe you after this?" It felt as if her heart were being torn in two. "I want you out of my house. Now."

He bowed his head. All the fight seemed to go out of him. "Fine. I'll go. But you're wrong, Julie. I didn't use you."

"Sure." She refused to believe him. He was no different than any other man she'd liked. She was a magnet for deceitful men, and Noah was no exception.

He did look so alone standing there. He didn't argue or lose his temper. She saw the regret on his handsome face before he turned, grabbed his coat and walked out her door.

Good riddance. The last thing she needed was a spying, suspicious man out to use her.

And she'd mistaken him for a friend.

"Noah, is that you, dear boy?" Nanna called out from the living room.

"Yes, but I could be anyone since you don't keep your door locked." Noah shut the door behind him. The cold had leaked into his bones, and he felt as if he'd never get warm. Plunging his hands in his coat pockets, he wandered into the hallway. "Want anything from the kitchen?"

"I have all I need."

Did she have to sound so happy? As if she had the answers to everything? She probably did, but that didn't help his situation. He'd messed up the first friendship he'd made in a long time. He felt guilty.

"Did Julie get ahold of you? She called here looking for you this morning."

Noah yanked open the refrigerator. "I met up with her in town."

"Good. She's such a nice girl, don't you think?"

Sure. And he'd made her nice and mad. He felt horrible. He'd hurt her.

"See that Crock-Pot simmering on the counter? I made a nice beef stew. We'll eat in a bit." Nanna was unstoppable. "Don't you go spoiling your supper."

He grabbed a carton of milk. "I'll be good."

"You will be, because I'm watching you, young man." Heels tapped on hardwood as she approached, all smile and charm. "You look much healthier after one day in my care. See what good, clean Montana air can do?"

"I know where you're going with this." He stole a glass from the cupboard. "You think I'm looking for business property."

"In case you decide to relocate." She handed him a clean glass. "It never hurts to keep your options open. Who knows? You might decide you love it here and never want to leave.''

"Yeah, sure, right after I find a bride. Neither one is going to happen. Trust me.''

"You think you know everything, young man. You just wait. The love bug is going to bite you hard. You'll be helpless against it.''

"The love bug? I graduated magna cum laude from Harvard and never once did I learn about the love bug concept.'' He filled the glass. "It must not be an academically recognized term.''

"I should never have spared the rod with you.'' She pinched his earlobe and held on tight, but it was an affectionate hold. "You are accompanying me to church tomorrow, aren't you? I have to show off my handsome grandson to all my friends at the Ladies' Aid.''

"I'd be honored. It's not every day I get to escort such a beautiful lady to church.''

"Oh, you take after your grandfather, boy. A charmer to the core, he was. And ambitious, too.'' She released him, only to fish a handful of cookies from the ceramic jar. "About tomorrow. Will I need to give you a talking-to?''

He kissed her cheek and stole the cookies. "I already know what you're going to say. I'll be nice to Harold. I'll turn off my cell phone in church. I'll go to bed early.''

"That wasn't what I was going to say, smarty.'' She patted the back of his hand, not willing to let him go upstairs, where his computer and e-mail were waiting. "It's so good to see you here. I love you so very much."

"I love you, too, Nanna." He hugged her tight and didn't want to let go.

But the Crock-Pot bubbled and the oven timer buzzed. She spun away to grab her oven mitt. Outside, dusk began stealing the daylight from the sky, but inside the kitchen, and in his heart, it was warm and bright.

Chapter Eight

It was just her luck. The first person she saw the exact second she stepped foot inside the church was Noah. He was standing in the aisle next to his grandmother and three of her friends. He shook each woman's hand, giving Nanna a kiss on the cheek. Winning their hearts, no doubt.

Yesterday, he'd been busy winning hers. Determined not to let it bother her, she tucked her purse strap higher up on her shoulder and lifted her chin. If she sat far enough in the back, she probably wouldn't be able to see him through the entire service.

Especially if she slumped down in the pew.

"Julie!" Susan scrambled up the aisle from the door. "Come help me figure out where he's going to sit."

Hopefully in the front row. "I was planning to hide out in the back."

"What for? You'll never be able to see him that way."

Julie opened her mouth to argue, but it was too late. Susan had spotted Misty, in the middle of the church, who was waving to catch their attention.

"I saved the best spot for us," Misty whispered breathlessly as they crowded onto the bench, a stone's throw from where Noah stood, still busily charming those kind, unsuspecting ladies.

"A perfect view," Susan agreed.

Too perfect. Julie deliberately kept her back to him. Noah wasn't her friend. He'd used her, and that hurt. She still didn't understand it. He'd seemed so nice. Kind, funny and wonderful. Unbelievably wonderful. She'd been up half the night, tossing and turning, troubled by his betrayal.

"Ooh, he's looking this way." Misty was nearly bursting with excitement. "Quick, smile and wave."

Julie couldn't resist a quick look at him, but she most certainly was not going to smile and wave. She felt his gaze like a bitter wind in her direction. Her heart ached, remembering his touch, his steady kindness, the way she'd sparkled on the inside when he said her name.

The aisle between them felt as wide as the Grand Canyon. Yesterday had changed everything for him, too. There was no easy grin on his face when his gaze met hers. He looked uncomfortable and sad. So was she.

"Wow, to think we danced with him." Misty leaned close, whispering to keep from being overheard. "He keeps looking our way."

"Mesmerized by the two of us. *Not* Julie." Susan winked.

"That's right. It's a shame how he ignores her. *Not.*" Misty winked. "I don't think he sees anyone else in the entire church."

Oh, no. Julie covered her face with her hands. "Is he really watching me?"

"Oh, yeah." Noah's voice at her ear, and his touch on her sleeve. "My grandmother wanted me to invite you and your friends to come sit with us."

He did look contrite, and that made it easier to be civil. "Thank you, but my friends and I are fine right where we are."

"Julie!" Susan admonished.

"Julie, please," Misty whispered.

Noah's eyes glinted with amusement. "Yeah, Julie. Please. I promise I'll behave."

"I don't care if you behave. I'm not budging."

"You're mad at me, I know. You have the right. But maybe you could put our differences aside for an hour, for my grandmother's sake. Would it help if I let you kick me in the shin? Flog me with the hymnal?"

"I'd like that. Do you want to stand up? Or should I kick you from here?"

"Ouch. I guess you're serious. Okay, I'll take the flogging. I deserve it. I was bad. Can you forgive me?"

"Not if you paid me." She wanted to, but he'd used her to get information on her grandfather. He'd found a private detective to dig into Granddad's life. "You can't charm me. I'm immune to it."

"I'm not," Susan spoke up.

"Thank you." Noah flashed the grin that could dazzle a shopping mall full of women in half a second. "You don't have to forgive me, Julie. You can jab me with your elbow through the entire service until my ribs are bruised. You can drop the hymnal on my toe until it swells and I can't take off my shoe. You can fire death-ray glares of disapproval at me for the rest of my life, but please, reconsider. My grandmother really wants you to join her."

"Maybe you should explain to her why I don't want to sit anywhere near you."

"Let's not. She'd get mad at me."

Julie was weakening. Noah could sense it. Victory was close at hand. "You don't want to disappoint your granddad. He's over there, sitting next to Nanna. See him? And what about your friends?"

Bingo. He'd used the right leverage. Her knuckles turned white, she was gripping her purse so hard. Good, because he wanted the chance to make things right with her. She was a good person. One of the nicest he'd ever known. He wanted to apologize. And he'd keep apologizing until she forgave him.

"All right," she relented. "But I want this perfectly clear. I'm not happy with you."

"I can accept those terms of our peace accord." He winked at her, hoping it would make her smile.

Utter failure, but he'd keep working at it. He wanted to clear up this misunderstanding. He refused to lose Julie as a friend.

He led the way across the aisle and made sure he scooted next to her on the hard wooden bench. Her friends crowded on his other side, but they were nice enough and he didn't mind chatting with them for a few minutes. As long as he could feel the solid heat of Julie's arm pressed against his.

"Stop trying to change my opinion of you," she informed him. "Making nice to my friends isn't going to make me dislike you less."

"Then I'll have to try another tact. Did you hear? Today's sermon is on forgiveness."

Her jaw snapped closed and she glared straight ahead. She looked mad at him, but her mouth was crinkled in the corners, as if she were fighting to keep ahold of her anger.

Yep, she was weakening. He was thankful.

Julie set the brim-full gravy boat on the corner of Nora's dining room table. It was impossible to keep from noticing the man on the other side of the table, setting knives and forks and spoons in place around the pretty china plates. Harder still to ignore the charming grin that he was sending her way.

He was trying to soften her up, and it wasn't going to work. Nothing on this green earth could make her forget what he'd done. He could wink, he could smile, he could dance on the ceiling for all she cared, and better than Fred Astaire, but it wouldn't change what he'd done.

Or how foolish she'd been.

"Did you enjoy today's sermon?" he asked. "I enjoyed it immensely. Made me really decide to reevaluate the grudges I've been holding against people."

"Really? I don't see anything wrong with holding resentment and hostility toward a person, if they truly deserve it," she quipped.

"That's not what I got out of the sermon."

"You must not have been paying attention." She turned on her heel.

She'd taken Pastor Bill's sermon to heart, and it was troubling her. Noah had hurt her, and yet, she didn't want to hold a grudge, didn't want to let the sun set on her anger. What should she do? Maybe the Lord would guide her.

"Just in time." Nora laid a thick slice of old-fashioned ham on the heaping platter. "If you take this for me, I'll grab the bowl of potatoes and we should be ready to eat, dear."

"Thank you for inviting us over." Julie took the platter, eager to help. "I'm glad you're marrying my granddad. He loves you so much."

"As I love him." Nora looked like the happiest

woman in Montana as she fished a hot pad out of a drawer.

Granddad lumbered into the room, his boots knelling on the hardwood, his hands jammed into his pockets. He looked uncomfortable. "Smells awful good in here. Need any help?"

Julie took one look at him, then at Nora's loving expression. She could take a hint. "I'll leave you two lovebirds alone."

She grabbed the bowl of potatoes, too. Granddad looked smitten as he stood there in the center of the room. Yep, they definitely needed to be alone.

She found Noah was halfway around the dining room table, doling out forks, spoons and knives like cards in a Go Fish game. "Hey. Have you forgiven me yet?"

"I need to hold on to my grudge until dinner's over, at the very earliest."

"Will that be before or after dessert? I just want to know how much time I have to perfect my apology to you."

"I hope it's a well-thought-out apology. A glib one is likely to make me toss a potato at you." She set the heavy platter and bowl in the center of the table. "I'm a pretty good aim."

"I remember. But I'm not afraid, because I've got a killer apology prepared." Noah sidled close to slide the last set of silverware into place. "I'm enjoying this, you know."

"I've noticed. Maybe I should pelt you with potatoes right now because it's not nice to hurt people's feelings.''

"I know, and I deserve it. You might want to lash me with a few ham slices while you're at it," Noah joked, because he knew he could wear her down. Soon he'd have her laughing.

She was so close, he could smell the strawberry shampoo in her hair. It was nothing at all to reach out and brush his knuckles down the side of her face, his fingers tangling in her hair. Petal-soft skin, and satin-soft curls.

Her eyes widened like a doe caught in a semi's headlights. "I'd better go check on Granddad. He—"

"They need their privacy, just as we do." He didn't want her to go. "I hate that I hurt you. Absolutely hate it."

"Me, too."

Pain was there, revealed in the dark shadows of her eyes, and he had to fix it. Had to repair every bit of harm he'd caused her. He had to tell her what lay in his heart. "I've had a lot of people betray me, Julie. People I trusted, and who were close to me. When I heard my grandmother was getting married, I feared the worst. Because I've had the worst happen to me once too often."

"And that's why you hired the private detective?" Julie's jaw looked tighter. "You couldn't come here with an open mind and decide for yourself, after meeting Granddad?"

"I can see you're getting angry again." He sighed. "Look, I don't want you mad at me. I like you. I want you to like me. I just need you to understand."

"I don't understand." She yanked open the drawer on the big glass cabinet thingy on the wall. The glass windows rattled. Silverware chimed. She grabbed a spoon and dug it into the potato bowl. She plunged a ladle into the gravy.

Good going, Noah. Looks like you messed that up.

"Good, you're both here." Nanna clipped into the room, carrying a basket of bread, sounding unusually strained.

That worried him. Maybe she was tired. He took the basket from her. "Let me get your chair for you. I love coming to a beautiful woman's assistance."

"You can stop laying it on so thick, young man, and ask Julie what she'll have to drink. I forgot the lemonade pitcher—" She snapped her fingers. "I just don't know what's come over me today. I'm forgetting everything."

"That's because a woman in love has a lot on her mind. It's perfectly natural." He kissed his grandmother's cheek, courteous and adoring, before he helped her scoot in her chair.

Julie's heart melted. Right when she'd been ready to stay mad at him, he had to go and do something like this. So sweet and affectionate, he made it impossible to stay mad at him.

Noah returned to the room with a pitcher of lemonade. Granddad followed him in and took a seat, cleared his throat. Nora said grace. After a round of "amens," Granddad lifted the bowl of peas and passed them to Julie.

It was so quiet. Nora was busy ladling gravy on her potatoes. Granddad spent a lot of time breaking a roll apart and buttering it. Not a word was spoken.

There was definitely something wrong. Nora and Granddad refused to meet gazes as Noah offered them each a first shot at the ham platter.

"Julie?" He nudged the meat-laden platter across the table. He lifted one brow as if asking a question, then looked at their grandparents seated at opposite ends of the table. About as far apart as they could be.

"Thanks." She forked a slice onto her plate, and gave him a shrug. She didn't know what was going on.

"Noah, I got a chance to speak with your sister after the service." His grandmother didn't look up as she broke the silence. Her voice sounded strained. "She couldn't come over—one of the little boys has an earache, poor dear—but she does want to drive you to the airport tomorrow."

"Goin' back so soon?" Granddad asked.

What about the doctor? Julie bit her tongue before she could ask the question out loud. She knew Noah wouldn't want his grandmother to know.

A chair scraped against the wood floor as Nora straightened in her seat. "We can just ask him, Harold. Noah, we have a meeting with the builder tomorrow. Now, it's a lot for us to take in. Why, I've lived in this house for most of my life. Harold is sure of himself, but, well, I would feel better if you sat in on the meeting with us.''

Julie watched Noah's face fall. She knew there was still the matter of the doctor's call.

''You really need me, huh?'' He glanced at Harold, then back at his grandmother.

Granddad looked surprised. ''Why, I won't say we need you, but it would make your grandmother happy.''

''I may as well leave a little later. Sure. I'd be happy to.''

''Oh, I feel better already.'' Nora looked relieved as she cut into a slice of homemade bread. ''It's such a big project. Our own home, together. It's a new start for us, isn't it, Harold?''

''Yes it is, sweetheart—'' Harold blushed, apparently embarrassed by his feelings.

Noah was starting to like the man. As if Julie realized it, she lifted one brow in a question. So, she was still blaming him, was she? Still angry?

He'd have to fix that, and quick.

''Harold, come help me with the tea water.'' Nora took her dessert plate with her as she rose from the table.

''Sure thing, honey.'' Granddad grabbed his plate and headed after her.

Julie blinked as they disappeared from sight. "Do you know what that was about?"

"No, but I think they want to be alone." Noah rubbed his brow, because this was too much. "Okay, I'm starting to see it for myself. Harold really does love her."

"You've taken care of her for a long while. It has to be hard to let someone else take over. He'll be good to her."

"I'm figuring that out."

"Didn't need an investigator's report for that, huh?"

"Not this time. I already admitted I was wrong."

"I heard you." Julie snared her plate and rose from her chair.

"I didn't use you. That's what you think, isn't it?" His dark gaze searched hers, forthright and unflinching. Beneath the steel was tenderness.

Julie's chest tightened. Her throat ached. What did she do now? She stared at her plate, no longer hungry, but it was a better place to focus her attention than Noah. She was no longer angry with him. It would be easier if she was.

"I know. I chose the wrong words. I do that sometimes."

"You're a billionaire. You're a chairman of the board. You're supposed to know what words to use."

"Sure, rub it in." He took the plate from her, his fingertips lingering over hers. Masculine and warm and amazing. "I'm just a man."

He walked away, leaving his confession to echo in the shadows. Just a man, he'd said. A man who made mistakes and apologized for them. A man who'd asked for her forgiveness.

She found him in the living room, where the fire was crackling in the fireplace and the cheerful atmosphere seemed at odds with their mood.

Noah hadn't touched the thick slice of chocolate cake on his plate. He didn't look up, not even when she settled onto the couch next to him.

She set her plate on the coffee table. "Going back home tomorrow?"

"Yep. I've got a meeting that I'll do by telephone. Probably on the jet on my way home."

"I always do tons of phone calls on my Learjet, too. It's a time-saver."

The tiniest hint of a grin tugged at the corner of his mouth. "I've always thought so."

"If the doctor does get ahold of you on your plane, then you'll be alone. You need your family with you, or your friends."

He relaxed a little, trouble starting to twinkle in his eyes. "I prefer being alone. It's easier than having women get mad at you right and left."

"That's your own fault, buster. Why haven't you told your grandmother? She would want to be there for you."

"Because there's nothing really wrong, that's why. I'm not going to upset her for no reason."

He seemed so sure of himself, but Julie wasn't

fooled. Not by a long shot. She'd seen his face change. He didn't like being alone any more than she did. Most of all, he didn't want to be seriously ill and alone.

"I saw you in the emergency room. I witnessed how much pain you were in—"

"It was nothing," he interrupted, holding up one hand to stop her. "Look how good I'm doing. I feel great. My chest hasn't hurt since we went skiing. If something were really wrong, it wouldn't have vanished like that. I had fun, exercised and, surprise, no pain."

"Have you ever heard of a fool's paradise? Of the ignorant's bliss? You should tell your grandmother and stay here until you hear from the doctor."

"Why? I think those tests are going to come up negative, for whatever it is the doctors are looking for. I live a stressful life. Stressful enough that it's made me unhappy for a long time. I just need to make some changes, that's all. The attack I had was some sort of wake-up call."

"I hope so." She truly did, but she couldn't shake the bad feeling deep inside. "I hope you're never in that kind of pain again."

"You care about me, huh?"

"I thought we were friends."

"We are." His hand covered hers. "A lot of people I know want something from me. A job, a better job, a loan, a wedding ring and no prenuptial. I learned to keep to myself. It's easier on the heart."

"I know what you mean, about protecting your heart." Her confession came rough as she twined her fingers through his bigger ones, holding on. "That's the reason I've vowed never to let myself think about finding a man to love me. It only leads to disaster, and my heart can't take much more breaking."

"I heard about the ring you returned," he confessed.

"Everyone knows. That's the problem with being left at the altar. The church is full of people who can't help but notice the groom's missing." She tried to make light of it.

He heard the pain anyway. "What kind of man would leave you at the altar?"

"He was a fertilizer salesman."

"You dated a man who sold fertilizer? I'm not even going to comment on that."

"He was nice to me. I thought that was enough. I just thought…" She looked so vulnerable and alone. Her ponytail brushed the slender column of her neck, so dark against her soft skin. "He didn't love me, and his best man told me so. In front of half the town."

Noah gently squeezed her fingers, offering her comfort. "What kind of man couldn't love you? Wait, don't answer that."

"A fertilizer salesman." She swiped dark tendrils out of her eyes, sad and trying not to be. "It still hurts. Maybe worse because it wasn't the first time."

"Someone else jilted you at the altar?"

"No, but I did have two other broken engagements, and I don't want to talk about them." Her eyes were glassy, as if she were holding back tears. She yanked her fingers from his and leaned forward and away, breaking contact and all the connection between them. She grabbed his plate and thrust it at him.

Heartbreak. He knew how deep it cut, how much it hurt. He could imagine her in a pretty white gown of satin and lace, alone in that crowded church. Abandoned by the man who'd said he loved her. She didn't deserve that.

"What about you?" Her silver fork scraped on the china.

"Love and I don't mix."

"Ever?"

"I tried it once, but I didn't have any better luck than you did." He speared a piece of frosted cake and chewed. He refused to discuss what had happened the one time he'd been weak enough, and foolish, to fall in love.

"Hey, I told you my heartache. You ought to be as brave."

"It's not a matter of courage. It just doesn't matter."

"If it hurt you, it matters."

She meant it. It was there in her eyes. "I came out all right, so don't worry about me."

"I don't like the way that sounds." She licked the frosting off her fork. "What are you? In your mid-thirties, and you've never been married. Do you have that fear of commitment thing?''

"Not me. I'm about as committed as a man can get. I work twenty-hour days, six days a week. Just about every day of the year. That's responsibility.''

"You're rich. Why do you work so much? I mean, you could retire. Then you'd have lots of time to spend with your girlfriends. You know, the ones you've got dangling on a string, pining away for you.''

"Is this your roundabout way of asking if I do a lot of dating?''

"Your social life is none of my business. I'm just saying…'' Her face was burning hot. She didn't want to think about Noah and dating. He'd go for a wealthy, sophisticated woman. The sort who wore designer labels and who wouldn't be caught dead in a pair of department store sneakers.

"I saw the way the women at the party were ogling you. You were magnetic.''

"It had nothing to do with me and everything to do with my bank account. As nice as your friends are, they don't see me. Who I am. What I stand for. If I were a poor man, they'd never look at me twice.''

His sadness touched her. "Some woman really hurt you, didn't she?''

"I'm not going to talk about it.''

Whatever happened, she sensed he had been hurt worse than she had in life. Tenderness filled her up, tenderness she didn't have the right to feel. Tomorrow he'd be jetting away in his plane to the East Coast, where he ran one of the most successful companies in the country.

And she'd return to her classroom that smelled of crayons and finger paint and chocolate chip cookies.

A teapot whistled in the kitchen down the hall, and Julie could just make out the low rumble of her grandfather's chuckle.

"They're so happy," she whispered. "It's adorable."

Noah didn't answer. "You have faith in marriage, do you?"

"Marriage is no different from life, I figure. It's what you make of it. Are you worried that your grandmother is going to be unhappy? My granddad will do anything it takes to make her happy."

"She's had one good marriage. I guess that means she knows how to make another good one. Marriage seems perilous to me."

"Me, too, and I've only been as far as the altar," she quipped, making light of the feelings she was too afraid to acknowledge.

Two sets of footsteps padded down the hall and into the dining room. The faint creak of a chair told her the happy couple was sitting down to enjoy their tea and conversation. The low, contented buzz of their conversation filled the house with their happiness.

Noah put his empty plate on the coffee table. The clink of the silverware on china echoed in the quiet.

He looked weary as he climbed to his feet and paced to the fire. "Want to know why I really hired that detective?"

She set her plate aside and moved close, so they could keep their voices low. "Does this have to do with the woman who broke your heart?"

"She did more than that." He crouched in front of the fire, staring into the flames.

Why would anyone hurt this man? Julie hunkered down on the floor and waited for Noah to say more.

"Her name was Vanessa and she went to my church. Still does, actually." He curled up next to her. "Sure you want to hear this?"

"Do you want to talk about it?"

"I never talk about it." He hung his head, dark shocks tumbling forward to hide his face. "But I need you to understand. I'm a man who would never mean to hurt anyone, and I feel bad about the P.I."

"I'm beginning to know that about you."

"Good. I hired the detective because that's what I should have done for myself, about five years ago. I trusted someone I shouldn't. Vanessa was kind and beautiful and seemed to understand me. I was lonely, and many of my friends were married, some happily. I thought, maybe that could be me, with a gentle wife who loved me. I really wanted someone to love me. Foolish, I guess."

"What's wrong with wanting to love and be loved?" Julie took his bigger hand in hers. Held him tight, so he would know that he wasn't alone.

He slipped his arm around her shoulders, drawing her close. Tenderly, sweetly.

How could anyone not love this man?

"Your parents divorced, as mine did. You have to know what it's like. The fighting. The conflict. The constant hurting. Words become weapons that hurt more than fists."

"Yes." She knew exactly what he meant. "But not every marriage is like that."

"That's what I told myself. I figured Vanessa was as nice as could be. Soft-spoken. Gentle. She never had an unkind word to say to me. Unlike you, she never showed her anger with me. That should have been a clue, in retrospect."

"What does that mean? You liked that I became angry with you?"

"You were honest with me. You were angry. There's nothing wrong with that. She hid every honest emotion from me, and I didn't know it. I thought no discord, no problems. I couldn't have been more wrong. She was sleeping with another man—my best friend."

"Noah, I'm sorry she betrayed you."

"I'm a Christian. I respect my faith. I wasn't sleeping with her. I guess that made it easier for her to pretend to be in love with me. When I proposed, I gave her a five-carat flawless diamond for an engagement ring and pledged to her my undying love. I was a fool." He'd lost more than his heart that day.

"I'm so sorry. You didn't deserve that." Julie wrapped her arms around him, in comfort and friendship.

He buried his face in her shoulder, her sweater soft against his skin, and held her. Held her, gently and gratefully, until the hurt deep in his soul ebbed away.

Chapter Nine

Noah padded down the hallway, following the single light shining in the dark house. "Nanna? Are you down here?"

"Just finishing up my reading." Nanna glanced over the top of her bifocals at him, from her place at the small kitchen table. Her Bible was open before her. "I thought I told you to get to bed early, young man."

"I was on my computer. Lost track of time." Noah turned a wood chair around and swung onto the seat. Getting comfortable, he leaned his forearms on the chair back. "Aren't you up pretty late?"

"Seems I have too much on my mind to fall asleep easy these days." Nanna swiped her hands over her face, looking weary. So very weary. "Between the wedding and the new house. It's a balancing act, I tell you. Hope and Julie are helping me with every-thing, but some days I can't stop worrying if my dress will arrive on time. Oh, and now the meeting with the builder.''

"I'll be there, Nanna. I'll help you as much as I can.''

"I know you will. Oh, I'm not complaining. I just need another cup of chamomile tea and to spend a few more peaceful moments with my reading.'' She touched her Bible. "What about you? Will you be flying off in that jet of yours the moment our little meeting is over?''

"You know I have to get back to work. If there's anything more I can do while I'm here, I'll do it.''

"My dear boy, one day, you are going to realize what you're missing in life. Then you'll stop working every waking hour of the day. You'll be running to your family instead of away.''

Her words hit their mark. Noah looked away. It was easier to stare at the floor than at the understand-ing on his grandmother's face. "I've been the cause of this discord between you and Harold. I should have been more welcoming to him.''

"You were polite.''

"You're defending me, and I love you for it. But you're right. We both know it.''

He thought of the story he'd told Julie tonight. The truth he'd never told anyone else, except for his at-torney. Not even Nanna understood the true reason why he couldn't stomach the idea of marrying.

He'd closed off his heart so completely, he couldn't let himself trust the people he loved. People who had never let him down.

He should confess. He should tell her about the stress attacks. They were over now, and he'd make sure it stayed that way. Nothing would cast a shadow over her upcoming wedding....

"You're the sunshine of my life." Nanna caught hold of his hand, her grip strong and faithful, loving and loyal. "It would be a great help to me if you'd give me your opinion of the construction bid. You and Harold could look it over together. Why, it would give you the perfect chance to get to know one another."

"So, everything really is all right?" He worried about her. He couldn't help it. "You were pretty upset."

"I know, but Harold gave me his word that he'd try harder. Now I'll need the same from you."

"Ah, you know I will."

"Fine, then, enough said. The meeting with the builder is at nine sharp. I know I'll make the right decision with my two favorite men to help me. I'm so pleased that you decided to change your plans out of your love for me."

"Bribery. Guilt. Manipulation." He kissed her cheek. "I didn't have any choice, but I don't mind."

"That's my dear boy." She caught his cheek and gave him a pinch. "Now off to bed with you. It's far too late as it is. Go. Scoot."

He stood and swung the chair into place. How could he tell her about those stress attacks, or whatever they were? She'd be worrying about the doctor and when he'd be calling and what he might say, during her meeting with the builder. A woman didn't get a new house, custom-built, every day.

It was only a stress attack. It wasn't as if it would be happening again. There was no need to tell her. Problem solved.

Noah's story troubled Julie most of the night. She woke up thinking about him, as the morning dawned bitterly cold. She had failed relationships that hurt to this day, but nothing like that. No wonder he'd given up trusting in people.

Well, he could trust her.

She added him to her morning prayers, hoping for a good answer from the doctor. He had looked healthier last night, almost as if the painful attack had never happened. Maybe Noah was right—it was stress. He certainly had a stressful lifestyle.

Snow began falling on the way to school. By the time she reached town to grab her morning latte at the coffee shop, the roads were slick. School buses with chains on their tires clunked down the main street, heading out on their routes.

"Hey!" Susan popped into Julie's classroom, her own latte in hand. "How was Sunday dinner with Mr. Billionaire?"

It felt private, all that had happened between her and Noah. "Fine."

"Fine? Misty and I have a theory." She tapped into the room with complete confidence. "Mr. Ashton the Third is sweet on you."

"On me? No, we're friends. And before you say one more word, remember that he lives in New York City. I live in Montana. And it's not only the miles that separate us."

"Aha! I knew it. You like him, too, or you wouldn't have thought this out so much. Admit it."

"His grandmother is marrying my grandfather. We have to be nice to each other. It's like a rule." Julie searched through the file folder open on her desk for the bright red *H*. "I'm a potato farmer's daughter. I have nothing but a string of failed relationships, so I don't think that makes me a prime candidate for a relationship with a wealthy, handsome and perfect man like Noah."

Susan nodded sagely. "Perfect, huh? Well, I guess that means he's available, after all. You don't mind if Misty or I try to charm him the next time he's in town."

"Go right ahead. Neither of you are victims of romantic doom." She grabbed the stapler and attached the *A* in place above the friendly-looking snowman.

"Sure that you're not feeling a little jealous? A little possessive?"

"No, why should I?" Julie stapled a *P* next to the *A*.

"Can we say the word *denial?* C'mon, Julie. You forget who you're talking to. I was standing right beside you when Keith told us that Chet decided not to marry you. I stayed with you when you cried long into the night. I sent back the wedding gifts for you, so you wouldn't have to face doing it. I know how much that hurt."

"You're a great friend, Susan. The best." Julie stared at the stapler in her hand, feeling lost and confused. "I know what you're going to say. You're going to tell me that I should take a risk again. That being jilted once doesn't guarantee it will happen again."

"So? What's holding you back?"

Julie thought of Noah. Of all the wonderful things he was. How he treated her. How much fun they'd had together skiing. How he'd apologized to her when he was wrong, and he opened up to her later. He told her his most painful secret. He held her in his arms, just held her.

"Noah is not the right man for me." She couldn't afford to let him be.

But that didn't stop her from thinking about him after school, when her room was quiet and silence echoed in the hallway as she closed her classroom door behind her. Had he heard from the doctor? Was he back home in New York by now and going about his normal life?

"Julie, I sure enjoyed the engagement party," the principal's secretary called the minute Julie stepped foot inside the front office. "I haven't had that much fun in ages. Your granddad sure looked happy."

"He is, thanks. I'm glad you had a good time." Julie looked in her box—the usual stuff—and jammed the paper into her book bag.

"My favorite part was seeing you dance with the billionaire," her cousin, Jenna, commented from behind a nearby computer. "Is there something going on? I had to help keep an eye on the caterers because you ran off with him."

"I'm pleading the Fifth."

"You took him to the hospital, didn't you? My brother saw you two in the hallway. He's an EMT, remember?" Jenna nodded sagely. "I bet Mr. Ashton was injured rescuing the little Corey girl."

"He's quite the hero," the secretary agreed. "Isn't that him waiting out there by your car, Julie?"

Every head in the office turned toward the window that looked over the lawn to the parking lot. Sure enough, there was Noah leaning against her truck fender. What was he still doing here?

His smile was genuine when he noticed she was marching across the grass in his direction. She had no idea what he was doing there, but he looked good doing it. He could have been a page torn from a men's fashion magazine with the way his longer black coat was unbuttoned to show a glimpse of the black suit beneath and a matching silk tie. He looked like a man who didn't belong in this small Montana town.

"Hey, beautiful. I saw the school buses pulling down the street and all the kids running down the sidewalk, and I figured you might be through with work for the day." He stole her heavy book bag and carried it for her. "Can I bum a ride from you? I need to get to the airport."

"What happened to your sister? Wasn't she going to take you?"

"Her little boy's earache is worse, so I told her to stay home. Nanna and Harold met with the builder today and dragged me along. I escaped after we'd gone over the contract, but they're still talking over the finer details of the house. Since I don't have a car, I'm stranded. So, here I am, hoping some pretty lady will take pity on me."

"It's your lucky day. I have an available vehicle, and I happen to have the rest of the afternoon free. You look good, so I take it the morning brought good news. What did the doctor say?"

"He hasn't called yet." Noah opened the truck door for her. "He's been stuck in surgery all day, but his nurse swore an oath that he would call me before four."

"It's been a tough wait?"

"No. I don't think it's bad news. It's just the waiting so I can hear those words for sure." He took her elbow to help her into the truck. "I don't want to be an imposition. Do you mind playing taxi for me?"

"Not at all. That's what friends are for."

"Thanks." He shut the door for her, pure gentleman.

She liked him, far too much. Good thing she didn't have to worry about a romance developing between them. And if a part of her wondered what it would be like to be in love with Noah, she would simply ignore it.

He hopped in the passenger door and tucked her book bag on the floor. "I'm sure your granddad will tell you all about it, but he and Nanna have finally settled on a house plan. They break ground as soon as the weather changes. I looked over the contract for them, that's why I'm staying in town longer than I planned."

She started the engine and backed out of the spot. "How did it go?"

"With your granddad, you mean? Well enough. I think he was glad enough to have someone who could read contracts for them." A shrill jingle sounded from his coat pocket. He tossed her a slightly worried look as he fished out the phone.

Hadn't he distinctly said he wasn't worried?

"I can do this." He took a deep breath, released it and punched a button. "Hello?"

Julie pulled up against the curb in the residential district. With the engine idling, she could hear the mumble of the doctor's voice.

"I see." Noah sounded…different. Strained. "Of course. I'll think about it. Thanks."

Her heart felt as if it stopped beating. Her blood turned to ice. The news wasn't good. Noah had turned completely pale as he punched the button that turned off the phone.

He was so silent. She wanted more than anything for him to turn to her and say, "The tests came out perfect." Anything to put the color back in his face and to sweep away the lines digging into his brow. This was not good news at all.

She didn't know what to say. No words came to mind, so she reached across the small distance between them to touch his sleeve. Noah didn't acknowledge her touch as he gazed out the side window. Snow tumbled in fluffy pieces to melt on the hood and cling to the windshield.

"I really thought it was nothing." He sounded so far away. "I'd talked myself into it. Nothing but denial, I suppose. After you took me skiing, I felt so great. I thought I'd dodged a bullet, that nothing was really wrong. If I started working out more and taking some time off, that would do the trick."

"What did the doctor say?"

"They found a suspicious mass in my abdomen." He felt wooden. Shock coursed through his veins, turning his blood to ice.

Tumor. He couldn't say the word aloud to Julie. Cancer at the worst. Gallstones at the least. The doctors wouldn't know until it was removed, and that meant surgery.

He buried his face in his hands. How could this be happening to him? It couldn't. The scans had to be wrong. He felt fine. He felt healthier than he had in years. It couldn't be cancer. Look at how he'd reduced his stress for one afternoon and the pain disappeared. That had to mean he was going to be all right. Right?

Lord, please let the tests be wrong.

He knew deep down they were not. The doctor wouldn't have called until he was certain.

"Noah, I'm so sorry. Did they say anything else?"

"Only that I had to have it removed as soon as possible."

"Do they know if it's benign?"

He shook his head. She was asking in a polite way if he had cancer, and he couldn't say that word out loud. What if it was that serious? He might be looking at the end of his life.

It couldn't be that bad, could it? This couldn't be happening to him.

"We can pray that it's benign. Will that help?"

He nodded. Her hand on his sleeve was the only thing that felt real right now. His head was spinning. His heart was thundering. But the steady warmth of her hand was like a connection that kept him grounded, that kept him from panicking. Her words were soothing as she began to pray.

He bowed his head, hardly able to hear her through

the rush of his pulse. The gentle words of her prayer reminded him that whatever happened, the Lord was watching over him. He would be all right.

He took a deep breath, calmer, stronger. *Thank you for Julie,* he added silently to the prayer before he murmured his amen.

He opened his eyes. Julie's face was all he could see. Her dark hair escaping in wispy tendrils from the ponytail to frame her face. The curve of her cheek, the light of her spirit in her eyes, the delicate cut of her chin that made him reach out and cup her jaw in the palm of his hand.

"Your friendship is the best blessing I've received in a long while." He'd never spoken so honestly. Overwhelmed with tenderness, he brushed his lips to her cheek. Sweetness filled him, and he felt heartened. Uplifted.

"You're a blessing to me, too." Her voice came rough with emotion.

He rubbed his thumb across the soft line of her jaw. She was so amazing to him. He'd never met anyone like her, so full of convictions and life and spirit. The caring that shone in her eyes seemed genuine. It really did. That amazed him, too, because he didn't see it very often.

"Do you want me to take you back to your grandmother?" she offered.

"No, I'm not ready for that, and I don't want her to know right now."

"I don't think you should be alone. I can call your

sister. Or, I know, I could take you skiing again. Or
we could just go to my place and talk. I'll even make
hot chocolate. We'll do whatever you need, Noah.''

His instincts told him to be sensible. He didn't
need to talk. He didn't need anyone. His jet was waiting. They were expecting him at the office. While he
was sitting here, work was piling up on his desks.
There would be memos, phone calls, e-mails and
faxes all needing his attention, and more problems to
solve than the day was long.

He had every reason to ask her to take him to the
airport.

Only one reason to stay.

She was waiting for an answer, half in and half
out of her seat belt, her sweater rumpled and a blue
paint smear on her sleeve. His thoughts should be
focused on the doctor's news. His emotions centered
on the fear or panic or whatever it was that he was
going to feel once the numbness and shock wore off.

Instead, he wanted to go skiing with her. They'd
had so much fun. No one had ever teased him like
that. And she'd raced him, and beat him. Man, he'd
had a great time.

The wind gusted against the side of the truck,
rocking the vehicle just enough to jostle him out of
his thoughts. A lot of snow had fallen, he was only
now noticing, and it completely covered the windshield except for a tiny row at the top. Giving him a
glimpse of the white-mantled maple overhead and

the ice-gray sky above. The sight of that sky made him yearn for something he couldn't name.

Or maybe it was this feeling Julie was creating in him.

Logic told him he had to leave. There was work waiting for him. It was the responsible thing to do. But that wasn't the real reason.

"I have to get back." He hated seeing the flash of disappointment on her beautiful face. He'd let her down, and he hadn't meant to. "Can I call you sometime, just to talk, friend to friend?"

"Absolutely. I should give you my e-mail address, too." She went to reach for her book bag, as if nothing were wrong, as if he hadn't just rejected her.

He pulled a card from his pocket. "Here's mine. Call me anytime, Julie. I mean that."

"That goes both ways." She ran her thumb over the embossed letters on the thin business card. "We're still friends, right?"

"Very good friends." He really liked her. He liked that she understood about romantic doom, since he'd had a lot of that in his life. He loved that she was his friend.

Out of the blue, he needed her, and she was there. She had to be a gift from heaven, a blessing wrapped up in a blue jacket and topped with a rainbow-striped cap. She'd reminded him there was more to life than work. Maybe even more to him.

What if this was cancer? He stopped his thoughts right there. One step at a time. He needed to contact a doctor back home. There would be appointments and surgery and… His stomach clenched tight with fear. He really didn't want to think about what happened then.

What mattered was the present. This moment. With Julie.

"Maybe next time I'll take you skiing." Yes, that's what he'd do. He loved skiing, and it *was* wintertime. Colorado was really something this time of year.

"Next time, huh?" She climbed back into her seat belt, trouble twinkling in her eyes. "I could be persuaded to ski with you again. For the right price."

"Wow. The right price, huh? How about a cup of hot chocolate?"

"Add marshmallows and you have a deal, mister."

How she made him shine inside, like the sun dawning in the dark night of his heart, bringing a fresh start and new possibilities.

He reached across the seat and twined his fingers through hers. He cared about her. How fortunate he was that she'd walked into his life.

At the small municipal airport, Julie watched Noah wave a final time before he disappeared behind the glass windows. The scent of his aftershave lingered in the cab and on her clothes. She felt lonely, knowing he was gone.

Way to go, Julie. You're starting to like him way

too much. And what good would come of that? Not one thing. Noah was rich, handsome, kind and a good Christian. Pretty much everything she'd ever dreamed of in a man.

As if he'd ever be interested in her.

Julie could see the small private planes through the security fencing. Without a doubt, she knew the pretty white-and-gold plane, the one that shouted "lavishly expensive" was Noah's. In a few minutes he'd be boarding that plane and probably settling down in seats of the finest leather. He'd snack on caviar and call Tokyo on his air phone.

Yep, she'd surely fit into his lifestyle. No problem. Her Chevy truck could compete with his jet anyday. So, she hadn't gone for the leather seats, and she didn't have satellite positioning. She could always upgrade, right?

Wrong. She shifted, pulling onto the highway. Snow scudded across the pavement, driven by the harsh wind. She felt like the road, laid bare by powers beyond her control. Her heart felt exposed, raw and aching.

He'd touched her. He'd been so sweet to her in the truck. Looking into his eyes, seeing the real Noah made her like him way too much.

It was his fault, for being so terrific, so gentle and kind and good and funny. He was to blame for going skiing with her and liking hot chocolate and caring so much for his grandmother. That would make any woman adore him.

He was at fault for being so wonderful.

Then he'd cupped her face with his big hand. "Your friendship is the best blessing I've received in a long while." And then he'd kissed her.

How had she let this happen? Wasn't being abandoned in front of her friends and family enough to prove to her that she'd always be alone? It didn't matter how wonderful everyone had been or how sympathetic and sorry, the truth was still the truth. Chet had tried to love her, and couldn't. He couldn't stand before God and take her as his wife. She wasn't someone he could love like that.

And Ray, the fiancé before that, had felt the same way. He'd fallen in love with one of her bridesmaids and they'd eloped. At least Ray had called her from Pocatello, Idaho, so she'd had time to cancel the wedding.

And her very first fiancé, when she'd been a tender nineteen, had been too young, just as she'd been. They'd made a mess of their romance because they had different values and different wishes for their lives. The breakup had been sensible, but it had left her feeling as if she wasn't good enough. That she'd never find a love of her own.

Three strikes, you're out. Isn't that the way it was? She often made light of it, but not even Susan or Misty or Granddad knew the real anguish in her soul. What was wrong with her, that love never worked out? That the men who said they loved her enough to offer her an engagement ring couldn't stick around? They, like her mother, didn't see enough in her to want to stay.

How on earth could she ever expect anything more from Noah? He had his choice of women, and he'd been horribly hurt in love, but…all you had to do was look at him. He was perfect in every way. When he chose to risk his heart again, it would probably be to fall in love with some slender, leggy supermodel, the kind that graduated from Harvard and launched her own charity foundation and did good deeds for humanity between photo shoots.

He deserved the best. Julie wanted that for him.

It was humbling and it hurt, but she was no supermodel, that was for sure. She merely had a teaching degree from the local university, and she hadn't graduated with honors. She wasn't photogenic, her charitable work was done through the church's annual food drive for the holidays and she'd be lost in a big city like New York.

And why was she even thinking like that? The man wasn't interested in her. He wasn't going to propose to her. He hadn't bought a tux for their wedding. He just wanted to go skiing again—that was all.

At the edge of town, she slowed to the posted twenty-five miles per hour, waving at the local sheriff, who was in his patrol car checking radar beside the road. They'd gone to school together, and his little boy was in her morning class. He saluted, as he always did, with a friendly smile. They'd dated briefly in high school. He'd been her date to Junior Prom. Now he was married and a father.

Some people were very blessed.

Feeling extralonely, she followed an impulse and pulled into an available parking spot in front of the town grocery. Tonight she would make Granddad's favorite meal and invite both him and Nora over for supper. Since she had her cell phone handy, she made a few calls to arrange it.

By the time she snagged her own cart from the front of the store and started through the aisles, she was feeling better. Her momentary lapse of sadness was gone. She had blessings she was immensely grateful for.

"Miss Renton! Mama, there's Miss Renton!" a little girl's voice rang out from the produce aisle.

Julie recognized a student from her afternoon class. "Hello, Brittany."

"We're shoppin' for the turkey." The little girl's ringlets bounced as she skipped to a stop in the middle of the aisle, leaving her mother's side and the brimming shopping cart. "Mommy's gonna make yams just the way I like 'em."

"With the sugary stuff?" Julie asked, as Brittany's mom bagged a head of lettuce before heading their way. "Those are my favorite kind of yams, too. Is your mommy baking a pie?"

"Three pies." Brittany held up the appropriate number of fingers. "My baby brother's too little to eat 'em."

"We're having the whole family over," Carol explained as she shoved the heavy cart to a stop, the new baby belted safely in the seat. "Oh, I had the best time at the engagement party. I haven't danced in so long and my feet still hurt from it, but I don't mind a bit."

"I'm glad you had a good time. How's your new baby?"

"Not sleeping through the nights, yet. Look, he's wearing the sleeper you gave him at the shower." Carol tugged down the blanket to show a blue romper. They chatted for a few more minutes, before Julie went on her way.

As she selected onions and bagged them, a baby began crying in the next aisle. Probably Carol's baby. The principal's wife whisked by with a basket and said hello, and later Julie waved at a friend from church in the bakery section. Kids were plastered in front of the glass display case of decorated cookies. Mothers were everywhere, hurrying to buy what they needed for supper, or shopping early for the upcoming holidays.

Julie checked off the last item on her list and headed for the checkout. She paid for her purchases, carried the two bags of groceries to her truck and headed home.

Alone.

Noah heard the phone ringing in the hall. Was it Julie? He didn't know why, but he hoped so. Maybe she'd call to see if he made it home safe. That would be just like her.

Hurrying as the phone continued to shrill, he punched off his security and raced through the room, dropping his keys and briefcase as he went. He couldn't wait to hear her voice.

He snatched up the phone in midring. "Hey."

"I'm mad as a wet hornet at you, young man," Nanna scolded. "You didn't tell me what happened, oh, no. I had to hear about my only grandson from my friends at the weekly Ladies' Aid meeting."

How had Nanna found out? Nobody knew about his test results. No one but Julie, and he hoped she hadn't told. How was he going to protect his grandmother from this? Her wedding was two weeks away, and he could be facing a cancer diagnosis. "Nanna, I'm sorry. I meant to tell you."

"Well, I should hope so. I asked Julie if it was true, when she invited Harold and me out to her lovely home for supper tonight, and she said it was. Whatever am I to do with you, my dear boy?"

"*Julie* told you?" He broke a little inside. He'd thought she was the kind of person he could trust.

"Trying to keep it a secret from your own grandmother. Don't you know how I like to brag about my Noah? Goodness' sake, how can I take pride in you if I'm always the last to know about your latest good deed?"

"Good deed?" Noah stopped in his tracks. Nanna

wasn't taking about the medical tests? Then what was this about?

"Saving that little girl from the creek. I heard how she was drowning and you dove in to save her." Nanna's voice radiated pride.

"Not true. The kid had fallen from her horse. Both Julie and I happened to be driving by when it happened. We stopped and found the girl in the field. We both took her home. End of story."

"Hmm, I didn't know that about Julie. She conveniently left that piece of information out of our conversation. Now I'm fed up with the both of you! Next time, you tell your grandmother what you've been up to. Do you hear me?"

"Loud and clear, ma'am. I promise I'll be good. So, you saw Julie tonight." Julie. He was glad she hadn't betrayed his trust.

"She cooked the most wonderful spaghetti sauce. I had to beg for the recipe from her. She baked bread and fixed up a fancy salad. My, it was a treat. She even made cheesecake for dessert. She's such a fine cook, I can't imagine why some man hasn't come along and snapped her up."

"Neither can I, Nanna." He rolled his eyes.

He loved his grandmother dearly, but she believed everyone should be married! Why? He'd never figure that out. Just because she had good fortune with her first marriage, she looked at love through rose-colored glasses. He adored that about her, but it wasn't realistic.

Although, to be honest, he liked to think people were happy together somewhere. That some marriages were about building one another up with love and caring. That was the kind of love television would have you believe. The trouble was, he'd seen the other side. He'd endured his parents' troubled marriage, and had the scars to prove it.

Chapter Ten

Julie couldn't sleep. She tossed off her down comforter and searched around on the floor for her fuzzy bunny slippers. She found them by touch and jammed her feet into them. Shivering, she groped in the dark for more clothing. She found a thick sweatshirt on the back of the chair in the corner and tugged it on over her flannel pajamas. The cat nestled in the chair cushion meowed his disapproval.

"Sorry, Wilbur." She rubbed his ears in apology and grabbed the book from the night table.

The wind whipped against the eaves. A storm must be blowing in. The downstairs was cold, too, and she headed straight to the kitchen. Popping a cup of water into the microwave took a second. In a few minutes, she had boiling hot peppermint tea steeping.

The cat slinked through the shadows to inspect his

food dish, just in case. He sat in front of his kitty bowl expectantly.

"It's not even close to breakfast time, and you know it." She tried to be firm with him, but he flicked his tail. Displeased with his human, Wilbur sauntered over to her and wound around her ankles, as sweet as can be.

"Turning on the charm, are you?" She lifted him into her arms to scratch him properly. He purred, leaning his chin against her fingers.

See, she wasn't alone. She had Wilbur. The happiness from the evening's dinner party seemed to remain in the kitchen, where Nora's hostess gift of silk flowers sat on the island, soft and colorful against the beige Formica. She had so many blessings, it felt wrong to wish for what she couldn't have.

Not knowing what to do, she carried her cat, her book and her steaming cup of tea to the living room. The fabric blinds were closed tight against the windows, blocking out the night and the draft. She hit the remote and the gas fireplace flared to life.

Wilbur, apparently having all the adoration he could tolerate, climbed onto his blanket and curled into a contented ball. Julie brushed the cat hair off her sleeve before flipping open her book. She would read, drink her tea—and in no time she'd be sleepy again. Insomnia wasn't going to trouble her for long.

Except she kept reading the same three lines over and over again. The inspirational romance that had kept her riveted an hour before bedtime couldn't hold her attention now. The words she kept staring at seemed to have no meaning. It wasn't the book, it was her. She *wanted* to think about Noah. She'd vowed *not* to think about Noah. And so she couldn't think of anything else.

If she closed her eyes, she could still feel his touch. His warm, steady hand cradling her chin. His feather-soft kiss on her cheek. She'd tried to forget the emotional closeness they'd shared, but it was impossible. All she had to do was think of him, and in her thoughts she was back in her truck, with his aftershave scenting the recirculated air and snow landing on the windshield.

I'm concerned about his health, that's all this is, she tried to tell herself. She would worry about anyone diagnosed with an abdominal tumor. But that wasn't the whole truth. She had so wanted Noah to stay with her, instead of leaving on his jet. She wished she had the chance to comfort him.

Okay, now that sounded a little selfish, and it wasn't how she meant it. She only knew that she wanted to mean something to him. She wished that when he was hurting, and when he needed someone to hold on to, he would reach for her.

But he'd gone back to New York. Returned to the world he preferred. He probably had tons of friends and an active life. Broadway plays and football games and museums to wander through on a rainy weekend afternoon.

It was a few minutes past midnight. It would be

just after two in the morning in New York. He'd be fast asleep, and in a few hours his alarm would go off and he'd start his day. It would be a day without her. A day when he wouldn't think of her once.

But she would think of him.

Noah couldn't sleep. He opened one eye to get a brief view of the clock—2:14, the green lights proclaimed. Great. He'd been asleep for an hour and two minutes. His chest was burning, and that wasn't a good sign. He prayed it wasn't the start of another attack. He had pain pills the doctor had prescribed for him, but he didn't want to take them.

Maybe what he needed was a glass of warm milk. With any luck, he was only experiencing heartburn. Indigestion. A pulled muscle between his ribs. Okay, he was reaching, but he was doing fine not thinking about the result of those tests.

If he didn't think about it, he didn't have to deal with it. If he didn't have to deal with it, then he wouldn't be afraid. He wouldn't wind up taking a look at what was really bothering him.

He figured staying in denial was a better alternative. He'd go along as he had, and in a few weeks his chauffeur would drive him to the hospital. With any luck, he'd be given anesthetics right away and he'd never have to think about the possibilities of cancer.

Cancer. Great, he'd been avoiding that word until now, and it made a cold fear wash him, from head to toe. He nearly dropped his robe on the floor. He couldn't find his slippers so he padded barefoot across the plush carpet, his step loud in the silence. A single sconce in the hallway guided him past a row of doors, all belonging to empty bedrooms, past the foyer and into the gourmet kitchen.

He hit the switch over the eating bar and the track lighting shone off polished stainless-steel appliances and marble countertops. The marble floor was cool on his bare feet as he trudged to the stainless-steel-fronted refrigerator and pulled out a gallon of milk. He tore the plastic loop and removed the cap. After locating a saucepan in the bottom cupboards, he set it on the stove.

Boy, the place felt empty tonight. His movements rattled around in the shadows, making the apartment feel enormous. Too big for just one person. He'd bought this place because it was a good investment and because it was close to work. That was before Vanessa, when he'd held out the smallest hope that he might get married one day and have kids of his own. A family that would fill the rooms with their laughter and toys and stuff to trip over in the hallway.

He hadn't thought of that in years, and it was because of those test results. The doctor had used the word *cancer*, and Noah felt as if the earth had fallen out from beneath his feet. Everything was uncertain. What would happen at his next doctor's appointment? How serious would the operation be? Would

he be able to return to his work? And his health…
Would he be all right? Or was this something so
serious, it would take his life? What if the time he
had left on this earth was much shorter than he
thought?

That was a scary notion. He'd spent the last decade
working long, hard days. Shouldering responsibilities
to the board, the stockholders and the employees who
received a check every two weeks. He'd given all he
had to this company, and there hadn't been much
time left for friends. Or family. Or doing anything
he might enjoy.

What if he had one year to live? How would he
spend it?

The milk bubbled, and he grabbed the pan from
the heat. He filled a porcelain mug. He'd work—
that's what he'd do. He'd put everything in order so
someone else could take over the responsibilities of
the company he'd built.

Work? No, that didn't seem like the right answer.
He carried the mug to the shadowed table. The light
over the sink cast a reflection on the black windows.
He hadn't bothered to pull the shades. Rain smeared
the glass, distorting his reflection.

He'd had a blast this weekend skiing with Julie.
Being out in those foothills, where the mountains
were so rugged and huge, they were close enough to
touch. That was paradise.

He loved skiing. He didn't go as often as he could.
And why was that? Because he was busy working

for a company that didn't care about him. That wouldn't miss him when he was gone and buried. Whether that was in a year or fifty years. He didn't love his company.

Trouble was, he didn't have a family of his own to love.

Sure, his sister and grandmother. But they were extended family. What he craved was a wife, kind in the way Julie was, who would love him and never let him down.

He'd never felt more alone than he did right now. Sure, he could pick up the phone and call Hope or Nanna. But Hope was married and truly happy. She had a husband and children, a real family of her own.

He couldn't tell Nanna about this tumor. Not after seeing her so happy this weekend. She and Harold had been adorable—there was no other word for it. The joy in her voice and the love in her eyes… No, he refused to take those away from her.

Maybe it was better this way. He really didn't need anyone. Really. This was supposed to be the best time of Nanna's life. He remembered how her face had lit with undiluted joy when she'd shown him the picture of her wedding dress. It has been light gray, beaded and embroidered and lacy—all the things a bride wanted. The bridesmaid dresses would be an emerald-green. She'd showed him that picture, too, of the simple and elegant dresses, exactly something Nanna would pick out to adorn her beautiful brides-maids.

Would Julie be one of them? He didn't know, but his thoughts turned to her. Maybe it was her presence he was missing tonight. The uncanny way she had of making him feel so deeply and so much. With her he felt real. As if his work and responsibilities vanished like smoke, and she was there. She'd been hurt, too. She knew what kind of scars a shattered relationship could leave.

He didn't know why she was the one. Why was it that she could simply sit with him in a snowstorm when he received the worst news of his life, and the constant aloneness he carried inside him disappeared.

What he wanted to do was to call her and hear the warmth of her voice. Julie was the only person he could talk to about this. The only one he trusted that much. It was past midnight in Montana. She'd be fast asleep, safe and at peace, tucked away in her cozy log home for the night. He couldn't wake her, but he wanted to.

That wasn't like him. He didn't need anyone, remember?

For the first time in his adult life, he felt off balance. As if someone had pulled the rug out from beneath his feet and left him to fall. In one moment on the phone with the doctor, his entire world had tipped on its side. Everything had changed.

He felt lost as the rain pattered against the windows and the wind gusted around the corner of the building. The warmed milk didn't soothe him. The thought of Julie only unsettled him. The burning pain in his chest was stronger. It hurt to breathe.

"When I am afraid, I will trust in you." The verse from Psalms came into his mind, and he felt comforted. Noah *did* trust the Lord to show him the way through this shadowed valley that had become his life.

Julie couldn't believe her eyes. There was Noah's e-mail address right there on her computer screen. He'd written! She clicked open the letter, not knowing what to expect. Now that he was back at home, surrounded by his friends and his busy life, she didn't expect him to think of her at all.

Wait a minute. Just because he'd dropped her an e-mail didn't mean he was feeling the same growing affection she felt. He'd probably typed a few lines in a friendly way. A short correspondence to a long-distance acquaintance. She shouldn't expect anything too personal or emotionally intimate.

"Dear Julie," she read. "I can't sleep and it's too late to call you, so I thought I'd write. I miss you."

She stopped reading and studied that sentence again. He missed her friendship? She certainly missed his. Her life felt empty without him. That didn't make any sense because she'd only known him for a short while. In their time together, he had made an impact on her heart.

"I meant what I said in the truck on the way to the airport. You've been a true friend."

A true friend, huh? Julie sighed. He kept using that word *friend*. Okay, she could take a hint. She knew he wasn't looking for love. Good thing, too, because neither was she.

Think of what a terrible complication it would be if he wanted to be more than good friends? Oh, he'd buy her gifts and ask her on dates. He'd be calling her and doting on her, and frankly, who needed that kind of attention?

No, she was better off sticking to being friends. A friend couldn't leave you at the altar. A friend couldn't offer you a dream of a happy family, only to snatch it away.

As for these bright, sparkling feelings growing stronger in her heart, it was platonic affection and nothing else. She refused to love one more man who was wrong for her.

"Dear Noah," Julie's e-mail began. "I hope you're enjoying your busy life in the city. Want to know what I did today? While you were probably in meetings in a room with hardly any windows, I was out on my skis. Enjoying nature. Watching the sun set into the snowcapped Rockies."

"You're torturing me." He twisted the top off the iced tea bottle and took a sip. He had been in meetings all morning and had spent the rest of the afternoon on the phone. Sure, he had a great view from his office, but what could compete with Julie's view?

And to think she could step off her back porch and start skiing, well, he would love to live like that.

And come to think of it, why wasn't he?

He ignored his assistant's knock at the door and the buzz of the telephone so he could keep reading.

"I had to keep out of the backcountry, because of avalanche warnings. We had a major storm blow through and dump a ton of snow. Maybe you'll want to schedule in a spare day when you come for the wedding. I'll take you up into the mountains and, trust me, you'll never want to leave."

She'd gone skiing—and had the nerve to write about it. Remembering the cool air rushing across his face, the exhilaration of gliding on untouched snow beneath mountains too beautiful to describe made the tension melt from his shoulders. The problems piled on his desk—messages and file folders and a heap of paperwork in the in basket—lost their importance.

"Noah?" Kate hesitated in the threshold. "There's a call from a doctor's office holding."

The surgeon? Cold fear washed over him, leaving him weak. Noah leaned back in his chair, took a deep breath and tried to calm down. It would be all right. Whatever happened, the Lord was with him. He wasn't alone.

He lifted the receiver. "Noah Ashton here."

"Mr. Ashton, this is Margie, Dr. Reynolds's nurse. We'll need to schedule a consultation this week. You'll have a chance to meet with your surgeon and go over the procedure. Looking at your blood tests, we can't rule out cancer. The doctor is quite concerned.''

''Yeah.'' That's what the Montana doctor had said, too. Suspecting cancer wasn't actually having cancer, but this time it was harder to rationalize it away. He'd been numb before, so the words hadn't really sunk in. Hearing ''abdominal mass'' had been enough to send him into a state of shock, but this…

Woodenly, he answered the nurse as best he could and scheduled an appointment, and then stepped into Kate's office to tell her to clear his Thursday afternoon.

''But that's the day you're leaving for Japan.'' She pushed back her glasses, frowning at her computer screen. ''Is this about the doctor's office? Is something wrong?''

He couldn't answer that. As much as he respected his assistant and how well she did her work, he liked things kept professional, not personal. Of course, if he *did* have a terminal illness, that would affect his professional life and everyone in it.

Don't think about it. He'd deal with that problem later. Right now, he had a takeover to handle, lenders to appease and the latest crisis that had taken up his entire day.

''Just clear the afternoon.'' He told Kate and headed straight out her door.

In fact, it was hard not to keep going. It was almost five. It wasn't an uncommon time of day for people to stop working and head home.

He dug in his heels to keep from marching straight down that hall to the elevator. A desk heaped with work was waiting, and it was his responsibility. He'd agreed to do it. Every person in this building was counting on him to run this company well and right. They had families to support, kids to raise, mortgages to pay.

And what did he have? Nothing. No one waiting for him. No family, no kids. The only person he'd let get close to him since his breakup with Vanessa was in Montana, probably finishing up her afternoon kindergarten class and getting more paint smudges on her clothes.

She may as well be a world away.

"If you're through with me for the day," Kate announced as she breezed by, carting a heavy briefcase, "I'm outta here. See you bright and early."

Was he really standing in the middle of the hallway, staring into space? He decided to do his ruminating in the privacy of his office.

Julie's note was still on his screen. It was amazing to him how much he missed her. He sat down at his desk, pushed aside the audit from the company he absolutely had to have three weeks ago and read the rest of her message.

Julie swept last night's powdery snowfall from her front steps. Saturday morning was still, the landscape sugary perfect. A deep mantle of snow hugged the world like a cozy blanket, and the only movement was a pair of bucks, wading through the drifts along her driveway.

The sun was slow to rise, casting long low fingers of golden light through the mountain peaks and across the glittering meadows. Perfect skiing weather, but she didn't feel up to it. Noah wouldn't be with her. She was a sad, sorry case, letting a man affect her like that. Without his companionship, not even skiing was the same.

Inside the house, the phone rang. Probably Granddad checking up on her. She'd cherish his concern for her while she could. Soon his life would be changing. He'd be married with little time to spare, which would be good for him. She suspected he called so often because he was lonely.

Leaving the broom on the porch, she shot in the door and snatched the receiver before he could hang up. "Good morning."

"Good morning to you," answered a familiar voice.

Not Granddad at all. "Noah! What are you doing calling me? I know you work on your weekends. Aren't you in the middle of a takeover or something?"

"I'm never too busy for you. I meant to answer your e-mail, but I decided to call instead. Are you going to torment me with more tales of your skiing adventures?"

"I could if you wanted me to." She didn't want

to tell him how her favorite thing to do on a winter's day now seemed to make her feel lonelier than ever.

How could she admit something like that to him? He probably had a busy day planned between work and friends and his city lifestyle. "I'm going downhill skiing at the Bridger Bowl, a few miles up the road, with Susan and Misty. What about you?"

Good question. Noah put his feet on the glass coffee table and leaned back in the leather sofa. What was he going to do today? The pile of work in his home office needed attention. He could always work out in the health club across the street until he forgot about the upcoming surgery he'd scheduled.

But he didn't want to tell her that. He would sound...pathetic, needy, like a man who didn't know what he wanted out of life. He didn't want to admit that to anyone, even Julie. "I've got a load of work to do. It'll keep me busy all day."

"Weren't you going to cut back on your stress?"

"Well, after I have control of this microchip company, I'll take it easy."

"I can tell when you're fibbing. I bet you're the kind of man who never takes it easy, even when your health is an issue. Is there a lesson here? What could it be, I wonder?"

"I'm going to do some relaxing tonight. Does that make you happy?"

"*You?* Relax? I don't believe it. Tell me the truth this time."

"I got some movies." He snatched up the DVD

cases from the bag on the floor. "Arnold's latest action adventure, and a subtitled one about crouching tigers that says right on the front it won a lot of awards. That ought to be good."

"You don't get out much, do you? Tell me you're as worldly as any other billionaire on this planet."

She was laughing at him! "I work a lot."

"You do get out of your office to go to movies, shows, plays. A museum now and then?"

"I mean to, but there's always something I have to do first."

"You could be living in a cardboard box and you wouldn't know the difference."

"Sure I would. A cardboard box would be drafty. I'd notice that." He felt a hundred times better hearing her voice, knowing her friendship was still there. "Remember the day I left for Montana? I promised that I'd take you skiing."

"Oh, so you have a few acres of mountain property?"

"Who doesn't have a few acres of mountain property?" He loved making her laugh. Her warm chuckle rumbled in his ear. "I have a cabin in the Rockies. I bought it a while ago thinking that I would start taking time off to do lots of skiing, but I was always too busy. I used to think I had plenty of time later to do the things I really wanted to do. Now I have to accept that I could be running out of time. If I want to do something, then I'd better do it."

He'd been wrong, hiding in his work for so long.

He was realizing it only now. How many days did he have left? How was he going to spend them?

Not sitting in his office, that was for certain.

He would savor every moment. He'd treasure every minute of being alive on this earth. God's gift of life was precious, and Noah was beginning to realize how much.

When Julie checked her e-mail the next morning, there was a new message from Noah. He'd listed a time and flight number. "I'll meet you on the slopes," he'd written.

The Colorado Rockies! Talk about exciting. She hadn't been out of state since she was in high school.

Noah hadn't given her much time. She'd have to talk to the principal, type up instructions for the substitute and pack. Pack? What did she have to wear? Okay, now she had to go shopping, too.

The cat flicked his tail in great disapproval when she sprinted up the stairs.

Oh, right. She'd have to ask Granddad to feed Wilbur while she was gone.

I'm going to Colorado, she wanted to shout out loud. The chance to go on a trip absolutely thrilled her.

And maybe the man did, too. Just a little, tiny bit. And only in a strictly *friendly* way.

Chapter Eleven

The first-class ticket waiting for her at the local airport should have been a clue. Even the limo waiting for her at the private airstrip in the posh skiing village should have made her stop and think, but she was too distracted by the incredible view and the impressive homes tucked into the mountainside. And knowing she was about to see Noah again didn't help.

She was blown away by the "little cabin" he owned. There was nothing little about it. Made of log and stone and glass, it blended perfectly with the surrounding forest. It was a picture from an architectural magazine come to life.

The limo rolled to a stop in the sloping driveway, and she couldn't move. She was still gaping, in awe of that house. Noah owned this. When he was sipping hot chocolate in her house and skiing on her land, he had almost seemed like any other guy. A really great guy, but still, as normal as could be.

This was not normal.

The etched-glass front door swung open, and there was Noah bounding down the inlaid stone steps to open her car door. He looked great in a dark blue sweater and jeans, his hair blowing up in the wind.

"Julie, it's good to see you." He said it so warmly, she knew he meant it.

He had missed her that much? As if in answer, he held his arms wide in welcome. She bolted to her feet and flew into his arms, feeling his solid chest against her cheek as he held her tenderly.

I missed you, too. She held back the words she didn't dare say. Her hands settled on his broad shoulders, and the wool of his sweater tickled her. Holding him like this felt right. Sweetness swept through her as gentle as a winter's dawn. She could stay like this forever, tucked in his arms, feeling his heartbeat against her cheek and be perfectly content.

But this was a friendly hug, she reminded herself, and stepped away from his embrace. "Little cabin, huh?"

"Well, I call it the cabin."

"As opposed to the penthouse and the Hawaii beach house?"

"No beach house, although I've always thought that would be a good investment."

"Yeah, me, too."

A dimple cut into his cheek as he grabbed her bags from the trunk. "Great. You brought your skis. Want to go grab lunch at the inn and then hit the slopes?"

"The *inn?* You mean that elaborate and expensive-looking hotel down the road?"

"It's just over the rise. We can ski there." He hefted her ski cases out of the trunk, acting as if this was completely normal.

For him, it probably was. Well, when in Rome... "Sure, let's ski over to the little inn down the road and grab a bite." Which probably meant filet mignon, lobster and caviar.

"This place has better skiing than Telluride." Noah manhandled her bags up the stairs. "Did you have a good flight?"

"It was a first-class seat. I don't think flying gets much better than that."

"Wait until you see my jet." He waggled his brows; it was the Noah she knew and loved. Okay, so he was rich. He was still a guy who loved his power toys.

But she saw the man. The real Noah who walked into a house where sounds echoed around him. There were no family pictures hung on the walls, no personal treasures stashed on the cherry wood shelves in the living room and not one favorite shirt slung over the back of the leather sofa.

They were not so different, the two of them, both living in houses with too many empty rooms.

* * *

He'd forgotten how sweet the air was at this altitude. Sweet enough to make his eyes sting, not from the cold but from something else. He didn't know what it was, but it made his chest ache deep.

He wasn't like this when he was alone. It was Julie. She was creating this feeling inside him. Her beauty, and her goodness and her friendship.

Who was he kidding? Friendship was too small of a word for what she was to him. She was like the only buoy in a storm-tossed sea to a lone survivor of a shipwreck.

"Hey, handsome. Are you ready to go?" Julie tugged her rainbow-colored cap down low over her ears, her poles waggling in the air.

"Where do you get a hat like that?" He tugged on the pom-pom on the top of her head.

"What's wrong with my hat? Okay, so it's not a designer one, like everyone else's. But at least it stays over my ears in the wind." She flashed him that smile, the one that made his heart lighten. "I bought it at the church bazaar. One of the women on the Ladies' Aid made it."

"I've never been to a church bazaar."

"You're one strange cookie, Noah Ashton." She lit up when she laughed, and made him brighten, too. "I suppose you buy your stuff from some ritzy tailor shop."

"No. I have a personal shopper."

"Oh, me, too. Doesn't everyone?"

"Are you laughing at me again? I suppose I deserve that for commenting on your hat. It's cute.'' It was Julie, bright and cheerful and sensible. In fact, he liked her hat so much, he grabbed it by the pom-pom and yanked it off her head.

"Hey, give that back!" She stumbled over her skis, swiping wind-tousled curls from her face.

Her lovely face that he wanted to gaze at forever.

"My ears are freezing. Noah!" She jumped, surprisingly agile on those skis, but she couldn't reach.

"You can have it when you catch me." He knew he was in trouble, because she could outski him, but he was no slouch. He double-poled, shooting onto the groomed trail. Soft snow powdered up behind him as he flew with Julie hot on his tails.

"You'll have to try harder," he taunted her, but didn't dare take the time to glance over his shoulder. He kept his concentration on the course, because she was on his heels. He could see the smudge of her blue jacket in his peripheral vision.

"Seemed to have overestimated your abilities, Ashton." She closed in on him, nudging around him like a thoroughbred going for a Triple Crown win. "Didn't think I could beat you twice, did you?"

"True. I thought your win last time was a fluke. Luck. Nothing more." He was breathing hard. Pushing hard. They were neck and neck.

"Nothing more, huh? Just luck?" She matched his pace, not even breathing hard. "Then explain this."

He saw her arm shoot out, and he yanked the rainbow-striped cap out of her reach just in time. The trouble was, she wasn't after her own hat.

He felt a tug on his head and a cold rush of wind over his ears. "Hey! That's mine. Give that back."

"Come and take it." She was off, kicking fast, leaving him in the dust.

He loved competition. He kicked hard, gliding far and fast on his newly waxed skis. She was still ahead of him, but not as distant. Come on, push harder, he coached himself. There was no way he was going to let Julie get away with his hat.

"Know what I think?" he called, his voice bouncing off the endless snow and miles of trees. "I think you have beginner's luck. That's why you keep winning."

"Ha! I'm no beginner. I've been skiing since I was four."

"You're a beginner. When it comes to competing with me." He was gaining, his strategy all along. "Got a little overconfident, did you?"

She was licked, and she knew it. They were neck and neck, stride for stride, hugging the narrow trail together. "The course is narrowing up ahead. It's getting steep, too."

"Really? I'm not afraid. I'm a downhill kind of man." He kept equal to her, although he had to work for it. "I've heard it's tricky up ahead. Skiers take a tumble all the time. Maybe you want to make a deal."

"There is something I want."

"Your cap." He was breathing hard, and his lungs burned from the cold. His legs felt as heavy as lead. He was more than happy to negotiate. "How about we call it a tie and trade hats?"

"That's a sensible solution, and it proves why you're successful in business." She wasn't winded, tossing him an easy, gorgeous smile that made him stumble.

A man couldn't look at a pretty woman and ski well at the same time. He kept his pace, but she eked ahead a few inches. He recognized that glint in her eye.

She was sure of success.

"I think I'll keep your hat," she informed him. "It *is* a designer label, after all."

"No way. I won't permit it." His ears were freezing, but that wasn't the worst part as she cut ahead of him, just out of his reach. He couldn't gain on her. He was doing his best, but he couldn't catch her.

The course tilted downward, the wind hit his ears and his skis glided across the snow like a dream. Exhilaration filled him as he stared down the face of the jagged mountain, the big slope miles wide and incredible. Not that he was paying much attention to it.

What was he looking at?

Julie as she glided down the slope ahead of him, taking the steep terrain like an expert. She was only a blur of blue through the blazing light and the glittering snow. She was grace and goodness, beauty and speed, and she filled his heart up in a way he didn't understand. She made his world tilt on end....

No, that was just his skis. He lost control, lost his balance and tumbled headlong into the powdery whiteness. He rolled, feeling the bindings give, and sat up, wiping snow out of his eyes.

"Are you okay?" Her angel's voice bounced across the expansive mountainside separating them.

"My ears are cold," he answered back.

It was clear she had no sympathy for him. She was busily adjusting his hat on top of her pretty head.

He was really starting to like her, more than he would ever have thought possible. She made him laugh and feel and ski full out on an incredible mountain slope until he felt alive. He was aware of every sense—the crumbling cold creeping down his neck, the fresh winter scent of the forest, the strange open sound of the mountains and the taste of snow on his tongue.

He'd never been so aware. Shaken, he managed to get back on his skis. Sure enough, Julie was still there, waiting for him, making certain he was okay.

Just as she always did.

"Hey, the last one to finish has to buy dinner tonight." Her confidence rang in her voice, in her stance, and he loved that. "A really nice dinner."

"Do I get my hat back?"

"I don't think so."

He loved a challenge. He pulled her cap on his

head. It was snug, but it felt like bliss against his freezing-cold ears.

Her laughter rang on the wind, light and merry. "I'm sorry. I shouldn't laugh. It's just…pom-poms aren't you, Noah."

"When a man has cold ears, he has to lower his pride a bit."

"A bit?" She doubled over, laughing.

Okay, she was going to be sorry now. He took off, full power, hitting the slope just right, sailing toward her before she could straighten up. Her last chuckle lingered in the chilly air as he soared past.

He had the advantage now, but he suspected not for long. When he glanced over his shoulder, there she was, gaining ground. He looked forward to the rest of the race.

And the finish.

The sun was sinking low between the snowy peaks, their jagged faces shot through with cool lemony light, making Julie squint as she trekked up the slope steep enough to need a rope tow. Every muscle she owned burned as if she'd been lit on fire from the inside. Her lungs hurt. Her feet felt like forty-pound dumbbells.

What she really wanted to do was collapse in a heap, let the cold snow cool her down and never move again.

"Slowing down a little?"

How did he still have enough energy to be saucy?

Ooh, she was gonna make him pay. Come suppertime, she'd order the most expensive thing on the menu.

Not that it would begin to put a dent in his wallet, but it was the principle of the thing. He'd tortured her every single yard of this marathon course. She couldn't let him get away without some sort of penalty, right?

"Careful. I'm catching up."

"It's those long legs of yours." She had to work twice as hard, and he was right there, trying to push past her. *Again.* She had to dig deeper and find just enough strength to keep ahead of him. Air rushed into her chest. A stitch dug into her left side. Her thigh muscles felt as wobbly as jelly.

No, she couldn't let him win! He was at her elbow, then pulling ahead as the trail end marker came into sight around the last bend. She couldn't do it. He nosed ahead, fighting just as hard, and the tip of his ski slid across the shadow made by the end post, a mere inch in front of hers.

"I can't believe I beat you." Panting heavily, Noah tumbled into the snow on his back. "I'll never move again, but, wow. I won."

"Yes, you did." His skis stuck up, in her way, and she skidded to a stop before colliding into him. "Congratulations, pom-pom man."

"Glad I've got your respect. I know I'm dashing in this hat. I'm gonna keep it." He was kidding, but he was charming and wonderful and made her happy, so she didn't care if she ever saw her hat again.

All she wanted was the man in it. She loved him. How could that be? She'd vowed not to love him, but the affection in her heart was too strong to hold back.

It was hard to keep the emotion from her voice as she held out her hand. "You look like you need some help."

"Thanks. I think I can move now." He sat up and climbed onto his skis under his own power. "You made me work for it. I haven't tried so hard since…" He shook his head, scattering powdery snow. "I can't remember when. I've won a free dinner. Wow."

"Wait, don't say it—"

"And I'm ordering the most expensive meal in the house," he interrupted. "Isn't that what you planned to do?"

"Me? Never. Well, maybe."

Laughing, victorious and exhausted, Noah led the way to the lodge. He felt so alive. And he knew whom to thank. So he helped her with her skis and let her choose a table close to the crackling fire.

"This place serves the best hot chocolate on the planet." He told her, as he tugged the pom-pom hat from his head. "And it's my treat."

"Oh, I thought the loser had to pay."

"Right, but even losers deserve chocolate." He kissed her cheek, light and sweet.

The sunshine streaming through the window seemed a little brighter when Julie smiled.

Armed with movies for their movie marathon, to be held in Noah's living room after dinner, Julie waited as he held the video store's heavy glass door. "I notice you're guarding the bag," Noah commented as he followed her onto the covered sidewalk. "Not a bad plan, considering if I accidentally misplaced those movies, then we could get those action flicks I wanted to see."

"I did offer, but you said losers deserved to pick out the movies. It's your own fault." She swung the plastic bag, sporting four movies. "Winners deserve to be tormented by chick flicks."

"Torture by romantic comedy. I think I can take it like a man." He winked, limping a little from their hard day on the snow.

"What's wrong with a little romance?"

"Not one thing." Trouble flickered in his eyes. "We've got a few minutes before our reservation. You sit right here."

"On that bench?" A cast-iron bench leaned against the wall of the florist shop. "No way. That is one cold bench. I'd be frozen solid in an hour if I sat there."

"Then stand here looking gorgeous." Noah brushed his lips against her cheek in a brief kiss, breathing in the strawberry scent of her hair and her skin. "I'll be right back."

"Ditching me already?"

"Not a chance of that. You wait and see." Because a woman who was buying him dinner deserved flowers, he stepped into the florist shop.

A bell jangled overhead, and a cheerful clerk stepped up to the counter. "Can I help you, sir?"

"What kind of roses do you have?" He waited while the clerk returned with samples of various roses. He considered the rich colors, yellow and red and pink and orange, but he kept going back to the white rose. Good and pure and true. It seemed the right choice.

While the clerk rang up the purchase, he could see Julie through the front window. She was leaning against a wood post, watching the activity on the street. The breeze had tangled her dark hair hopelessly and she looked…good and pure and true.

He took the flowers, wrapped in pink paper, and left. The bell jangled above the door, and Julie turned at the sound. He watched her gaze snap to the flowers.

Delight lit her up. "For me?"

"For the loveliest woman I know."

The delicate fragrance filled the air between them as she took the bouquet. The daylight was fading, shrouding them in blue-gray shadows. "Movies, compliments and flowers. It doesn't get much better than this."

"That's the idea." He brushed tangles from her face with his leather gloves, a gentle brush that made

Julie love him, again, a little bit more until there was nothing but the shining brightness of it, filling her up.

"Now," he said, steering her toward the finest restaurant in the village, "I'm getting hungry for my lobster dinner."

"Lobster? Sure you don't want bread and water?"

"As long as I'm with you, water would taste like hot chocolate." He resisted the urge to steal back his hat, for she was wearing it, and took her hand instead.

"Popcorn's ready," Noah called from downstairs. "How about you?"

"I'll be there in two seconds." Julie found her bunny slippers in the bottom of the suitcase she borrowed from Granddad and slipped her feet into them.

She felt like warm, melted butter from an hour spent in the hot tub. Her muscles had hurt something fierce when she'd tried to get up from the dinner table, so the jetted hot water was exactly what she needed.

It was so incredibly relaxing as they sat together in the huge Jacuzzi with the deliciously hot water bubbling between them. Sipping on lemon-flavored mineral water, they watched the full moon slip behind dark clouds. As they talked, snow began to fall. Big white flakes tumbled over them to melt in the steam.

So she was feeling better, and her favorite pair of

sweats felt like pure bliss on her skin. But it wasn't the time spent in the hot tub or the fabulous bedroom of Noah's sister's that she was in or the luxurious house or the sumptuous dinner of lobster and filet mignon. All the expensive and wonderful things in the world couldn't matter to her.

Just Noah. He made her feel this way. As if she were so happy, she would burst. As if there were so much love in her heart, it would lift her off the ground like a giant helium balloon. Every moment she spent with him made her love him more. Every time he made her laugh. Every time he smiled at her.

If only he loved her in return.

How was she going to hide her love for him? How could she go downstairs, sit on the couch at his side, share a bowl of popcorn and pretend that he was only her friend, just a skiing buddy?

I can do this. She paused at the door, pressed off the light switch and followed the row of elegant wall sconces to the wide, curving staircase. The sound of the television grew louder as she went. There, in the great room below, was Noah slipping a DVD into the player.

"Hey, you look ready to relax." Crouched on one knee, the lamplight burnished the wide span on his shoulders and the curve of his rugged face, a face that had become so dear to her. "Love the slippers."

"Thanks." She skipped down the stairs, keeping a tight hold of her heart. "The popcorn smells perfect. Light, fluffy. Buttery."

"Of course it's perfect. Did you have any doubts? I excel in many fields. Business. Computers. And the most important one of all, the fine art of popcorn popping." He held out his hand, palm up, inviting her close. "I used extra butter, just for you."

It was impossible to resist placing her hand on his. Her feet moved of their own volition, drawing her to him. She was hardly aware of settling down on the incredibly comfortable sofa or Noah moving away to dim the lights as the movie started. She could tell herself a thousand times that Noah Ashton wasn't the man for her. But it didn't matter. Not one bit. She still loved him.

"Lemon or raspberry?" He held out two chilled bottles of tea. "Wait, I bet you want raspberry. There are napkins on the coffee table. Go ahead and put your feet up on the coffee table. I do."

The leather made the softest rustle as he sat next to her. Not right next to her, but close enough to make her wish he would sit closer. If only she had the right to snuggle against his side and feel the weight of his arm across her shoulders.

Some dreams were simply not meant for her.

Every leg muscle Noah owned protested as he limped down the hall. Maybe his body was protesting the extremely early hour, but it was more likely the exertion from yesterday's skiing contest. Remembering the pleasant and companionable dinner Julie had bought him, made the pain worth it. He loved spending time with her, just talking about little things or nothing at all.

"Julie?" He rapped his knuckles against the paneled door. "Are you up?"

"My spirit is willing, but the rest of me isn't," came the muffled answer.

"Well, tell your spirit to drag the rest of you out here. We're running out of time." He knocked again. "Don't you want to help me realize one of my dreams?"

"No." There was a smile in the sound of her voice, if he wasn't mistaken. "No one has the right to dream after only four hours of sleep."

"Who needs sleep?" Their movie marathon had lasted well past midnight. "Do I have to come in there with a vat of cold water?"

"A vat, huh? That I'd like to see." The door opened, and she was there, dressed in jeans and a sweater. Her rainbow scarf was slung around her neck, and her hair was sleep tousled and wildly framing her face. "I'm ready and willing. I'm not sure about being able, but I'll try."

"Have a few sore muscles?"

"Why, do you?"

He limped after her. "About a hundred."

"Me, too." They limped down the hall together.

In the kitchen, he helped her slip into her warm jacket. The scent of strawberries clung faintly to the fabric and to the tousled strands of her hair. He found her mittens for her and knelt down to help her with her boots. His muscles protested, but he didn't mind. Any woman who'd get up with him this early in the morning deserved a little first-class treatment.

"A double latte with hazelnut flavoring, as you requested." He held out the insulated mug, the black plastic cover locked in place. "And one for me."

"You must want to get me out of the house pretty badly." She wrapped her scarf around her neck and worked her jacket's zipper up to her throat. "To help me with my boots and make my coffee."

"Yep. I've done this only once before, but I remember how fantastic it was. You wait and see. Getting up this early and halfway freezing to death is going to be worth it." He opened the door for her. "Trust me."

Trust him? She did. With all her heart.

The snow was crusty. The minus-degree temperatures felt bitterly cold on her face. She nudged the scarf so it covered her nose, and followed Noah down the icy steps and through the dark, silent trees.

"Careful. It's slick." Noah took her free hand, his fingers lacing through hers, holding her steady so she would not fall. "Look."

She couldn't see anything but him. He was her entire world, the dark rim of night and the stars winking out were nothing compared to the warm solid feel of his hand linked with hers. Then he gestured toward the eastern rim, where the faintest gray had replaced the inky blackness of night. The glacier-capped mountains glowed dark and mysterious.

Slowly the light changed. Gray became purple, then blue and crimson. Peach and pink crept over the horizon to brush subtle strokes across the cloudless sky and hushed peaks.

"This is what I wanted to see." Noah's voice came rough and raw, and he didn't bother to hide the emotion gleaming in his eyes. "This is the one thing I wanted to see one last time."

"You wanted to see the sun rise? Doesn't it do that every day in New York?"

"Just keep watching. I promise. It's going to be spectacular. A once-in-a-lifetime view." He whispered, because the peace of the morning strengthened, like a symphony's crescendo.

There. The first ray of golden light stabbed through the jagged peak of the lowest mountain. Bright, eye-stinging light that was bold enough to chase the darkness across the width of the sky. As if gathering courage, more light punched above the craggy peaks, illuminating the valleys and slopes of the mountains. All at once, the top curve of the sun thrust into the sky, changing the gray to blue and the shadowed world into a thousand shades of color.

"'The Lord is the light by which we see,'" Julie whispered.

"Yes. I thought of that verse, too." He tightened his grip on her, holding her tight, drawing her close.

Too many emotions warred deep within him to begin to name them all. He only knew that he was moved beyond words. That his faith in the Lord was stronger now. Strong enough to help him face the hardships ahead; powerful enough to be a light for his path.

"I saw this by accident on one of the few times I ever came here." He set his coffee on a boulder tucked into the slope behind them and took Julie's other hand. So small, so *right,* in his. "I was up early to make a conference call, and I saw this from the living room window. There was too much glare inside the house—I had the lights on—so I grabbed my coat, left the phone and went outside. I felt called to it. I don't know why...."

He held on to her so tightly. "I watched the sun rise into the sky like a promise of life, and I was too afraid to let it move through me and change me. So I went back inside and found the phone and picked up practically where I'd left off. I lived my life as if it had never happened. I don't want to make that mistake again. Whatever time I have left, I'm going to make count."

"Sounds like the right path." Julie heard the affection in her voice. The love she could no longer hide. It swept her away, lifted her up, so beautiful and infinite and true.

He had to know it. His eyes grew dark as he turned to her, reaching out. The first brush of his gloved fingertips felt like a dream against her cheek. He nudged her scarf down, so it drooped beneath her chin, exposing half her face to the crisp mountain air.

He's going to kiss me, she realized, and everything inside her stilled. It didn't seem real as he leaned forward, his gaze searching hers so deeply, she felt her soul stir. Felt as if he saw everything inside her, all her love, all her fears, all her needs.

Then his hand cupped her jaw tenderly, such a welcome touch, and his lips slanted over hers. His kiss was warm and gentle, as sure as a kept promise. She'd found her Prince Charming, the one man who could make her spirit complete and heal the broken places in her heart.

Noah's kiss was like a dream, something too precious and rare to be real. He didn't love her, of course. He was simply carried away by the moment and his regrets, that was all. She couldn't take this kiss seriously. She couldn't begin to start dreaming. Noah Ashton was never going to love her, never going to slip a wedding ring on her finger, never going to hold their baby in his arms. And why was this happening? Why was she wanting everything she could never have?

She broke away, quietly burying the love in her heart. Noah didn't want her, not truly. How could he?

Help me, Father. Please help me protect my heart. Help me to do this the right way. She *would* be strong.

Noah gazed down at her, his hand at her jaw, his emotions tender in his eyes, in his voice, in his touch. "What a beautiful way to start the day."

He broke her heart wide open with his words, and she couldn't speak. It struck her like the cold wind, and she felt it all the way to the marrow of her bones. She would love him. Always.

"Are you hungry?" Noah asked, as courteous as always. "Let's hike down to the inn."

"Sure."

It took all her courage to follow him down the trail past the house of wood and stone, as his *friend* and not as the woman who loved him.

Noah couldn't seem to make his hands stop shaking. Nothing like this had ever happened to him before. He folded the last sweater into his suitcase and went in search for the rest of his socks. Packing to leave wasn't what was important, but he felt as if he had to find every last sock. Maybe because it was easier to be unsettled over misplaced articles of clothing than the real, honest-to-goodness fact that he'd kissed Julie. A full-fledged kiss that continued to affect him—he glanced at the alarm clock by the bed—seventy-three minutes later.

She'd tasted like spun sugar, made him feel as bright as the sunrise, like a day newly dawning. Everything was changing around him—what he wanted, what he believed, what he'd always done to keep his heart safe. There was nothing to protect him from this ache in his heart. It wasn't from his medical condition, because that low burning pain was a daily occurrence, but this was something bigger and greater. Something he didn't understand. Something he had no success with.

He was in love with Julie Renton. The kneel-down-on-one-knee-and-propose kind of love. The love that came soul deep. It was more exhilarating than taking an ungroomed slope at full speed. What he'd felt for Vanessa was nothing compared to this.

He was in love for the first time.

Light footsteps padded down the hall. There she was, so beautiful he couldn't breathe, leaning against the doorframe, looking amazing in a pair of black jeans, riding boots and another of her fuzzy sweaters. This one was a soft yellow that brought out the luster of her porcelain skin and the rich red tones in her dark hair. It wasn't just her physical beauty that captivated him, but all of her—her goodness, her spirit, her faith.

"The limo's here." She winked at him. "That was really fun to say. I'm going to do it again. The limo is waiting for me. That's hysterical. I suppose the Learjet is, too?"

"You're having fun at my expense. I'm not sure I can permit that, not unless I make you pay." Forgetting the socks, he snapped the suitcase shut. "I'll have to keep your hat as compensation."

"It's a one-of-a-kind original. Ought to bring in a good bid at Sotheby's. Okay, maybe on eBay."

He loved that she made him laugh. To feel this way, to be this lucky, seemed too good to be true.

Chapter Twelve

I can do this, Julie vowed as the limo whisked them along the icy, narrow road past the village. I can keep this platonic. I can be the friend Noah needs.

He was talking on his phone—it had shrilled while the driver was stowing their bags in the trunk—and it sounded like a business crisis. On the seat beside her, dressed in jeans and an expensive green sweatshirt, he looked like the down-to-earth man she'd come to know so well. But his voice, dark and booming with authority, made it clear he was no ordinary man. He was powerful enough to run a multibillion-dollar company with ease.

"Sorry about that." He punched off the phone. "I'm heading back to Japan anyway, but now it's ASAP. I need to get this all squared away before my surgery."

"You're going to have jet lag going into the operating room."

"They'll give me an anesthetic, and I won't notice the time difference," he quipped, because she'd hit a nerve.

Then again, he was already on edge. The way he felt about her was new and overwhelming. He didn't know what to do about it. Did she love him back? Or did she feel only friendship for him? How did he figure out which, because he'd finally figured it out. He wanted more than friendship.

He loved her. Not just for today, but for always. He needed her. More than the life he'd built in New York. More than the money he'd made and the luxuries he enjoyed.

And because he loved her, he should tell her. Let her know how he felt. And how much he needed her by his side.

What if she didn't feel the same way?

What was he doing? He was a confirmed bachelor. Why were his thoughts running away from him? Why was he imagining a future that included love and marriage? He didn't believe marriage was a good thing. There were bad-luck marriage genes in his family. The only thing he'd ever failed at was love.

He was terrified. The thought of marriage scared him more than the possible cancer did. He couldn't make promises. He couldn't offer her a ring she might not want.

The one thing he would never allow is for Julie to

be as unhappy as his mother had been. That was what he knew of marriage, and just because Nanna and Hope had found joyful marriages, didn't mean he could.

No, he couldn't romance her. Besides, there was the surgery, and the possible cancer. He had to see how that turned out first.

So, now what? He had intended to ask Julie to come for his operation. He needed her by his side when he walked through the hospital doors. He wanted to know she would be waiting for him when he opened his eyes in his private room.

Was it wise to ask her?

His chest tightened. Pain seared through his lungs. Just another attack trying to gain strength. He took a deep breath and dug in his briefcase for his pain pills.

"How are you feeling? Do we need to take a detour to the hospital?" She didn't look at him when she said it.

"The pills have helped. I don't like to take them, but I haven't had a full-blown attack since Nanna's engagement party."

He took the pill without water, swallowing it down. He wanted the pain to subside.

"Look." She eased across to the far edge of the seat to peer out the tinted window. "There's your plane."

Was it his imagination, or did she feel so far away?

* * *

Julie gazed up at Noah's white-and-gold plane that looked as expensive as it had to be, glinting in the morning sun on perfectly groomed tarmac. She'd taken a commercial flight here, to Colorado, because Noah had been rushing back from Japan. Didn't he say there was a change of plans, that he had to return to Tokyo?

For some reason her feet slowed down. When he'd been with her in Montana, it was easy enough to pretend that he wasn't much different than she was. That he was an ordinary man. Yet, when she stepped into the shadow of that sleek jet, one of many on the tarmac, she could no longer deny the truth. Ordinary men drove pickups and didn't have vacation homes in the Rockies with a million-dollar view.

Above the whir of another small plane's engines rose a woman's voice. ''Yoo-hoo! Noah Ashton, is that you?''

A woman trotted into sight on heeled boots, her long legs encased in taupe leather. Her matching duster draped her perfectly. Diamonds winked at her throat, on her ears and on every finger, except her left ring finger. ''Noah! It is you. Where have you been? I haven't seen you since Daddy's birthday party, and you were there ten minutes before you slipped away.''

''Hi, Marley.'' Noah nodded a polite greeting. ''I'd like you to meet my friend Julie.''

Friend. There was that word again. And it hurt. It hurt to greet the gorgeous woman, who was really very nice. Julie learned that Marley was the daughter of the CFO of Noah's company. She was poised and graceful and had just returned from two months in Paris. She had a jet like Noah's, except it was red and white.

"It's very good to meet you, Julie." Marley's welcome seemed genuine. "Isn't the skiing here fantastic?"

"Absolutely. It's nice meeting you." She felt plain next to this woman who was so beautiful. Perfect from her rich blond hair to the tips of her polished designer boots. Yep, Julie definitely felt plain, and out of place, and that wasn't Marley's fault or Noah's.

"We're on a time schedule, but it was good seeing you, Marley," Noah said politely. "Tell your father he needs to call me."

"Sure thing. You know he'll be calling to see that I'm here safe and sound." She tapped away, waving her long, slender, perfectly manicured fingers. "Good seeing you, Noah," she called out, and was gone, followed by two men each pushing a huge cart of luggage.

Marley was the kind of woman Noah would marry one day. Julie wasn't jealous of that, no.

Just brokenhearted.

"Come on," Noah told her. "Let me show you my plane."

"You like your plane, do you?"

"Hardly at all." He held out his hand, taking her elbow to help her make the first step.

Always the gentleman. To his CFO's daughter, and to his friends. That's what she was—one of his friends. With each step Julie took, her hopes tumbled more and more until there was only a terrible sense of shame. What had she been thinking? Noah was never going to love her.

He needed a friend. He'd never said anything differently. As for the kiss, she'd misinterpreted that. He'd called her his friend often enough to make it clear. He wasn't going to fall in love with her.

And why would he? He was wealthy. Not just rich, but megawealthy. He would never want a country girl in jeans and a homemade sweater. He'd never marry a woman who wore a knit cap with a pompom on it bought for two dollars at the yearly church fund-raiser.

She'd asked the Lord for a sign, and He had answered her. He had shown her how very far apart Noah's world was from hers. The last thing she wanted was to fall in love with a man who couldn't love her in return. *Again.*

Tears burned in her eyes and blurred the lovely décor of Noah's plane. She knew he was coming up the steps behind her, and she had only seconds to pull herself together. To swallow her grief and her heartache and blink the bothersome tears from her eyes. To tuck away her dreams of what could never be.

He was a fine man. Her soul stilled at the sight of him. Wind-tousled like a pirate, as graceful as an athlete and powerful as the self-made man he was.

He would never be hers.

"You want anything to drink?" Noah grabbed a bottle of Perrier from the minibar. "I've got soda, tea, water. What's your pleasure, my lady?"

"You don't need to wait on me, thanks."

"It won't be long until we touch down in Bozeman. Think you're going to be able to walk out of here?" He made light talk as he crossed over to her. "I don't know about you, but my muscles are hurting. This fantastic skier I was with really pushed me to the limit."

"At least I won't be suffering alone." She tossed him a smile, dimpled and stunning.

That was the smile he wanted to see forever. He jerked his gaze away, staring out the window. He wished he could tell her how much he needed her. What this trip had meant to him. He wanted to open up to her so much that it hurt.

He took a long drink, staring out the window at the gray, misty clouds below. Jumping from the plane without a parachute would be less terrifying.

"Do you have a busy week ahead at school?" he asked instead, because that was easier. Keep the conversation light and on the surface.

"I'm on recess duty all week, and that's going to be a challenge with all the snow we've been having.

Snowball fights,'' she explained when Noah raised an eyebrow in question. ''One or two break out every recess to keep things interesting. Plus it's the last full week before Christmas vacation. The kids tend to be high-energy.''

''You love teaching, don't you? You light up when you talk about it.''

She wanted to tell him about her love of teaching, but what good would it do? Her chest felt so tight, it was hard to breathe. The truth was, he didn't love her. He was sitting here, so close she could reach out and kiss him if she wanted. He saw her as his skiing buddy. She couldn't keep doing this, pretending to be his friend. It tore her apart.

''I enjoy teaching. I wouldn't do anything else.'' That's right, keep it light. Don't let him know how much you're hurting. ''When I went to apply at the elementary school, the kindergarten teacher had suddenly retired. I was lucky.''

''Teaching kindergarten is a pretty competitive job, then?''

''Not like yours, but it can be, in the world of teaching.'' She averted her gaze and started digging through her purse.

Something was wrong. She seemed distant. There was no banter and no cute quips to make him chuckle. Noah picked the wrapper off the water bottle, wondering how to take this.

He ought to rejoice. After this weekend, she'd spent time with him, and realized she didn't like him.

Why else would she sit there, dragging a book from her purse, when they'd been close only this morning…

It was the kiss. While kissing her full on the lips had made him realize he loved her. It made her decide to put distance between them.

See? It was a good thing he was keeping his strictly bachelor status.

Julie didn't love him.

Pain tore at his chest, but it wasn't anything a pill could ease. It didn't make any sense, because hadn't he decided not to pursue a romance with her?

He tugged his computer from its protective case and hit the power button. Good thing he had work to do. Something else to concentrate on. To make himself useful.

But he couldn't concentrate. The numbers on the spreadsheet meant nothing, so he closed the document and opened Solitaire. He played the game, trying to pretend that he was all right when Julie was at his elbow, so beautiful and perfect. With her bouncy hair and her elegant profile and the way she bit her bottom lip when she thought.

She didn't look up once for the duration of the flight.

The forward momentum stopped, and Julie hit the buckle so fast, she couldn't hear the click as the seat belt released. She was on her feet, jamming her book into the depths of her purse.

"In a hurry, huh?" A muscle in his jaw jumped. "Wait two seconds. I want to thank you for a fun ski trip."

"It was fun." She'd had a great time, but not because of the skiing. Because of the man.

If she could, she'd pray for time to turn around and run backward and return them to Colorado. Where the air was thin and clear and the beauty breathtaking. She wanted to hold on to that time forever. The way Noah had laughed. How he'd looked wearing her hat. The cozy evening spent together watching movies.

But she had to move forward. Get back to the life she loved.

As hard as it was to descend those steps into the icy Montana wind, she did it. When her feet touched Montana ground, she'd never been so relieved. She'd done it. Finished this trip with her dignity intact. No one would ever know how close she'd come to making a big mistake.

"Hey, Julie!" Noah called, taking the steps two at a time. "I got something for you."

Not a present, she prayed. Please, not a memento of this trip.

"Thought you might need this, since it's a one-of-a-kind original." He held out her hat. "Whatever happens, at least I've seen the sun rise in the Rockies. Thank you for sharing that with me. So I didn't have to go alone."

She took a shaky breath, because that was all the

proof she would ever need. He hadn't wanted to be alone; that's why he'd invited her along. His words made her throat ache, and she hated that her hand trembled when she reached for the hat. "You take good care of yourself, and I'll be praying for you every night."

"I appreciate that. More than you know."

Then he was gone, climbing the steps into the jet, disappearing into the mist of snow and wind swirling around him, her Prince Charming in a white-and-gold Learjet.

Noah watched Montana fall away below as the jet climbed through the clouds. It felt as if he were falling, too, spiraling toward earth. His chest felt empty and hollow.

The more he thought about Julie's behavior, the more it troubled him. How could they go back to being friends after this? Every time he looked at her, he'd see the one woman he would always love.

Chapter Thirteen

I'm late. Late, late, late. Julie tossed a banana and a container of yogurt into her book bag. No time to cook breakfast. No time to pack a lunch. With the way her feet were dragging, and the new snowfall, she'd be lucky to get to school before her kids did.

Okay, keys? Check. Wallet? Check. Lights off? Check. Iron unplugged... She leaned around the corner to peer through the laundry room door. Check. Jacket? There it was, slung over the back of the chair, right where she left it after coming home from the ski trip.

She rushed through the back door, zipping her jacket as she went, wading through ankle-deep snow. There was a familiar green pickup parked to one side of her driveway, a plow attached to the front end.

There was Granddad shuffling through the snowfall, away from her open garage door. "I got your truck warming up. You're normally long gone by now."

She kissed his cheek. "I'm way behind this morning. You shouldn't be here clearing my drive. I have my own plow, you know."

"Keeps an old cowboy like me busy." He winked, jamming his hands into his coat pockets. "Did you have a good time on that skiing trip?"

"The best time." It hurt too much to think about. "What about you? Getting married next week. Are you nervous?"

"After all these years of bein' alone? I'm lookin' forward to it." He knuckled back his Stetson. "You have a good day, now."

"Want to come over for supper?"

"I'm eating at Nora's."

"Sure you are. I'm going to have to get used to that." She sprinted into her garage where her truck was waiting, the heater almost blowing tepid air.

She put the vehicle in gear and backed out of the garage. Alone, driving down the country road, the realization dawned. She was on her way to work. Her life would go on as it had. Nothing had changed. There was work and friends, and Sunday dinner with her family after church.

The only difference in her life was a big, yawning emptiness in her soul.

Her mother had left. Each man Julie committed her heart to changed his mind. Over the span of a lifetime, it was a message she heard loud and clear. But had she listened to it?

No. She'd gone right ahead and given her heart away a final time. She'd known better. She knew how it was going to turn out if she fell in love with Mr. Wrong.

And now look at her. Crying on the way to work when she could have protected herself. Could have turned down Noah's offer to go to Colorado. Could have turned away from his kiss. She could have thrown away his flowers instead of putting them in a vase in the middle of her table. Because a part of her couldn't stop wishing. Still.

Pulling to the side of the road, she let the pain wash over her, the horrible grief that broke like a dam. And she couldn't stop it. She didn't even try.

"Noah?" Kate rapped on the desk. "Earth to Noah. Did you want me to fax the documents?"

"Sure." He shook his head, realizing he'd been staring off into space. Again. He couldn't seem to keep his mind on anything.

The truth was, not even work was absorbing enough to distract him from the loneliness. It couldn't disguise the truth anymore. He was lonely and unhappy and a coward. He loved Julie. He couldn't stop thinking about her, couldn't stop daydreaming about her and replaying in his mind every second of every minute he'd spent with her.

"I'll cover your meeting in Washington tomorrow.'' Kate, efficient as always, tapped on her small handheld computer, studying the screen. ''Your notes are thorough, as always. I'll drop you an e-mail, let you know how it went. Hope your procedure goes well tomorrow.''

''Thanks.'' It was hard, knowing tomorrow would be a day of reckoning.

He was ready. There wasn't much he could do but face it head-on. And if he was scared, well, he knew whatever happened, he would be okay. His life, as it always had been, was in the Lord's hands.

There were last-minute calls to make. Loose ends to tie up so he could be gone for a few days. He tried to work hard, but his mind kept wandering and his heart wasn't in it. Being at this desk used to thrill him. Gave him a sense of purpose. Made him feel as if his life had some significance.

So, why did he suddenly feel as if he were trapped by four walls? As if he could never be happy unless he was zooming down a mountainside at full speed.

It was the skiing he missed, he insisted stubbornly. Vacations were bad things, see? It made a person not want to work as hard when the vacation was over.

It had nothing to do with Julie. So, she hadn't wanted him. She hadn't wanted his kiss. It was probably just as well. Think of the heartache a romance caused. And marriage…

His stomach twisted and his mind spun him backward to the dark of night in his bedroom, and the harsh, angry voices of his parents. The crash of a glass against a wall. Mom's furious litany of words that made him crawl out from beneath his baseball-motif bedspread and huddle on the floor in the corner, next to the giant-size teddy bear. He curled up tight.

He could smell the grass and dirt on his baseball cleats from the game. Dad hadn't made it. He had a meeting, like always. Mom hadn't come, either, but his game wasn't what they were fighting about. They were fighting about him. Mom wanted him out from underfoot because he demanded too much attention.

Pain tore through him like a thunderclap, bringing him back to the present. Back to the peace of his office, where the hum of the computer and the whir of the heating system were the only sounds. He was breathing hard, and sweat beaded on his forehead. *Lord, please make these memories stop.* But they remained there, like a shadow behind his thoughts for most of the afternoon.

By the end of the day, he couldn't take it anymore. Maybe the surgery was bothering him more than he thought—more than he was letting himself feel. One thing was certain, the past seemed too close, as if he could reach out and touch it. He worked late and grabbed takeout from his favorite deli on the way home.

His building was quiet, the security team reading the day's newspaper as he picked up his mail. Bills. Junk mail. A letter from Nanna.

Great. He'd been planning to call her tonight. He

wanted to know how the wedding plans were progressing and if her beautiful gown had arrived today as promised. Mostly, he just wanted to hear her voice before tomorrow. She was a great comfort to him.

The Lord had blessed him greatly in giving him such a fine, loving grandmother.

Why hadn't he really considered that before? The Lord had given him a loving grandmother and a loyal sister, and what did he do? Noah didn't trust anyone—not even God—with his heart. Not his grandmother or his sister. And not Julie.

He kept everyone at a distance, and the minute they got too close, off he went. Jetting away to Japan or New York, and never returning phone calls or e-mails. And why was that? Because of that memory he had today, that's why. That little boy rejected by his parents over and over again had grown up into a man who allowed no one to reject him.

Maybe there wasn't a bad-luck marriage gene. Only a man too afraid to love anyone completely.

In protecting his heart, he'd really been turning his back on some of the Lord's most important blessings. What kind of Christian did that make him? What kind of man?

Tomorrow he was facing surgery. When the doctors removed the tumor, they were going to test it for cancer. There would be no one in the waiting room, or in his hospital room or there to hold his hand while he waited for the lab results.

It wasn't what he wanted. He hated being alone.

He hated that he was afraid to depend on anyone. Worst of all, he was running out of time to change things. If he didn't do it now, then he might never have another chance.

He unlocked his door and marched straight to the phone.

"Miss Renton, I can't get this on." Emily trudged up to the edge of the desk and peered up at her, pleadingly. "Mommy said if I don't wear my mittens, I don't get Twinkies. They's my favorite."

"Mine, too. Let me see what's wrong here." Julie circled around her desk and knelt to inspect the problem. Emily's mom had sewn buttons to the sleeves in order to secure the mittens, and one mitten had come unbuttoned. "I can fix this. Stand still for me, okay?"

Disaster averted. With a smile, she sent Emily to the door to take her place in the lineup. When every kid was accounted for, coats buttoned and little backpacks claimed, she led them in double rows down the hallway and out to the loading zone where a half-dozen bright yellow buses waited patiently in the blowing wind and cold. A long line of cars hugged the curb behind the buses, full of mothers waiting for their children.

"Thanks, Miss Renton!" Emily skipped in the direction of the cars. Her black curls bounced in time with her gait. Her mittened hand reached out for her mother, a plump smiling woman who knelt down to take a look at the beautiful cotton-ball snowman her daughter had made.

"Bye-bye, Miss Renton!" Marc offered shyly, his cotton-ball snowman a boyish wad that looked more like a football than anything else. He had a mother, too, who balanced a baby on her hip, and who listened to him patiently while he led the way to their minivan.

Such lucky families. A yearning so strong nearly knocked her to her knees. She'd prayed for days now, trying to stop this ache in her heart. Why had God brought her down this path, just to break her heart? Why had Noah come into her life at all?

His surgery was tomorrow. Had it been a coincidence that she'd met Noah the same night his health came to a crisis? No, Julie didn't believe in coincidences, but she did believe in the Lord. And we know that God causes everything to work together for the good of those who love Him and are called by Him.

By turning away from Noah, was she stepping off the path God had made for her? What if this was God's will for her?

I don't know what to do, Lord. How had everything become so complicated? Was she turning her back on a friend? Or simply being realistic? How did she know?

When the last of her charges had safely boarded their buses, Julie turned heel and headed back inside. Susan caught up with her. Susan had blueberry muffins and was willing to share. She'd grab the bakery box and be right over.

Who could argue with blueberry muffins? Julie stopped by the teachers' lounge, grabbed two vanilla sodas from her stash in the back of the refrigerator, her contribution to the impromptu get-together.

Thankfully, the heat had kicked on and her room was toasty warm as she deposited the bottles on her worktable in back and grabbed an eraser from the chalk tray.

A ring came from inside her desk drawer. With chalk dust on her hands, she dug out her cell phone. "Hello?"

"Figured you'd be done teachin' your class by now." It was Granddad. "Are you sittin' down?"

"Close enough." Since she still had a hold of the eraser, she started cleaning the board. "What's up?"

"Got a call from Nora a few minutes ago. Seems that grandson of hers needs her to come out there, and she's askin' me to go with her."

"You should be at her side, Granddad." Julie kept her voice as steady as possible.

"You don't seem too surprised, girl. You've been spending time with that billionaire. Do you know what's going on?"

"Yes, I do." She hadn't realized she was holding her breath, but she felt tension melt away as she exhaled. She was glad Noah had told his family.

"Nora said to bring you along, if you can go. Her granddaughter is making the travel arrangements for us right now. Are you comin'? I suppose you were probably gonna be headin' out to be with him anyway?''

She heard the question in his voice. He was asking more than that—he wanted to know if she and Noah were romantically involved. "No, Granddad. Well, I wasn't sure."

"Then should I have Hope make a reservation for you?"

Yes, her heart said. But she couldn't go. He hadn't asked her to go. She couldn't fly out uninvited just because she was worried for him—no, afraid for him.

"It sure would mean a lot to Nora if you came," Granddad persisted. "Sounds like a pretty serious situation he's in. If somethin' were to go wrong, it wouldn't be right not to be there."

Exactly.

"I'll take care of my own reservation." There, it was decided. Julie promised she would ask the neighbor to look after Granddad's dog, and hung up.

She stared at her cell phone and the board she'd cleaned without noticing. Well, one dilemma solved. She was going to New York.

Noah heard them in the hall and yanked open the door. It was two in the morning, and he was in his robe and slippers, but he didn't care. Nanna led the way, with his sister on her heels. Harold was hauling luggage out of the elevator.

"Noah!" His grandmother pulled him into her

arms, holding him tight. "You shouldn't be up. Hope has a set of keys. The last thing I wanted to do was wake you at this hour."

"I haven't been able to sleep anyway, so I decided to wait for you." He didn't tell her that he'd spent hours poring over his Bible, trying to stay hopeful. That he had a thousand worries and more regrets. "Come in. Let me help with your luggage."

"Harold will handle it." Nanna's touch was a comfort as she took his hand, leading him toward the living room. "This place hasn't changed much since I've been here. There's no wife. No children."

"I found a matched set of a wife and kids at Bloomingdale's in my price range, but they clashed with the furniture so I took them back. Got a nice floor lamp instead."

"Very funny." Hope hugged him, too, holding him extra tight. "How are you? What time do you have to be at the hospital? Nanna and I have come to take charge of you, since you can't seem to take care of yourself."

"That's right," Nanna agreed like a no-nonsense general. "You'd better follow my orders, too, young man. You'll say hello and get to bed. Where do you want Harold to put the luggage?"

"Hello, son." Harold looked exhausted but stood as straight as ever, not weighed down too much by the luggage he carried. "You tell me where you want this."

"Down the hall, second door on your left." He

was surprised that Harold had come, too. They hadn't exactly gotten along. "It's good of you to be here."

"You're family now, or will be once I get your grandmother to wear my wedding ring. There's nowhere else I'd be." With that, he disappeared down the hall.

Okay, so Harold wasn't a bad guy, after all. Definitely good enough for Nanna.

"It's too late to scold you properly for not telling me about this sooner," Nanna scolded anyway. "So all I'm going to say is shame on you, and leave it at that. Now get to bed, because morning will be here before you know it. Hope, would you mind heating some tea water for me? I always get lost in that big fancy kitchen."

"Sure thing." Hope hugged him one last time, and he felt what she didn't say.

They were a family. They would stand by him no matter what the prognosis. They were there to lean on, if he needed them.

He'd spent the night with his Bible, preparing for the worst possible outcome. Now, with his family here, he was ready for the best.

Chapter Fourteen

"Julie." It was Hope Ashton Sheridan standing in the hallway, closing the door to Noah's hospital room. "I'm glad you made it. Noah's out of recovery. The mass was even bigger than they thought, and they wound up taking out his entire gallbladder, but he's doing great."

"Thank God." Julie hadn't realized how worried she'd been. No, *worried* wasn't the word. *Terrified.* "I wanted to be here earlier, but my flight was delayed. I'm just so thankful he's okay."

Her knees were strangely weak. She had to sit down. Stumbling, she made it into the nearby waiting room and found a chair. Her overnight bag slid from her shoulder and hit the floor. The tiny vase she held felt as if it were made of iron, so she set it on the nearby magazine table. Boy, was she shaky or what?

"I'm tired," she explained to Hope. "It was a tough flight."

"I understand." Was that sympathy in her eyes?

Okay, so that's one person I haven't fooled. Julie rubbed her hands over her face. "Is Nora in with him?"

"No. Harold made her go get a sandwich in the cafeteria. She's pretty worried about him. We all are."

Me, too. Julie bit back the words, not comfortable revealing more of her heart. "Is he awake?"

"Still sleeping. Why don't you go in and sit with him? I was on the way to make a call. I need to check in with my husband. Maybe you could cover for me until I come back?"

"Sure. Whatever you need." She could do it. She was Noah's friend. After all, wasn't she wise enough to keep control of her feelings—this time?

Clutching the bud vase, Julie gathered her courage, steeled her heart and stepped into the small room. It was quiet and dim. Noah was asleep on his back, his hair dark against the pillow. Several blankets covered his big masculine physique. Lying there so still, he looked vulnerable.

Oh, Noah. She flew to his side. Her fingers ached to brush across the high cut of his cheekbones and down his face to the strong line of his jaw. She yanked her hand back in time—he wasn't hers to touch.

Lord, please protect him and keep him safe, she prayed. *Because Noah is my heart.*

She leaned over him and pressed a kiss to his forehead. A featherlight brush of a kiss, so he wouldn't wake. Then she set the bud vase with the single bloom on the table where twenty other arrangements were crowded together. They were all elaborate, expensive bouquets, a few with colorful balloons swinging overhead. From friends, she figured.

Her single flower looked unimpressive and lonely. She almost snatched it back, but something seemed to whisper to her to leave it, so she did.

Then, after one final look, she walked out of Noah's room and closed the door behind her.

"Julie!" It was Noah's grandmother, leaving Granddad's side to rush down the hall. "Oh, did you hear the good news? It's not cancer."

"Are they sure?"

"Yes! Isn't that wonderful? Praise the Lord." Nora wrapped Julie into a tight, comforting, wonderful grandmotherly hug. "I am about to dance a jig of joy. My beloved grandson is going to make a full recovery!"

"I'm so thankful." Julie stepped away, trembling, and Nora pushed into the room. As the door closed, Julie could see the older woman settling into a chair at Noah's bedside, taking his hand in hers, tenderly.

Julie ached with gratitude. Tears stung her eyes. *Thank you, Lord, for sparing him, for holding Noah in the palm of Your hand.*

There was no need for her to stay. So she retrieved her overnight bag from the waiting room, said good-bye to her granddad and walked away.

"Julie?" Noah struggled away from a dream and opened his eyes. The wisps of the dream faded. Impressions of her presence, soft as a new day dawning. Of her kiss, gentle and reverent on his brow. Her scent of strawberries lingered faintly in the air. That was some powerful dream, he decided.

Someone was holding his hand. Nanna. He didn't need to turn his head to know it was her. He squeezed her fingers, and she held on so tightly.

His head was a little woozy and his vision fuzzy. He wasn't feeling so great, but the sight of her was like warm chocolate on a cold day. Okay, in truth, for a split second, with the scent of Julie's perfume in his memory, he'd dared to hope she'd be the one sitting at his bedside.

But Nanna was, and he loved her for it. She looked tired and drained. He was sorry for that, and he held on to her more tightly.

"Nanna, how are you? Are you—?" He squinted to bring her into better focus. Were there tears in her eyes?

It was bad news. He knew it. He felt it like a cold wave that rolled down his spine. *Help me make this easier for Nanna, Lord.* That was his first wish. Then he prayed for himself. *Help me not to waste another single moment I have left on this earth.*

"Oh, my dear boy. It's good to have you with us." Nanna scooted her chair closer.

"How can I sleep for long, with such a beautiful woman at my side? You look exhausted. Where's Harold? He's supposed to be taking care of you."

"He's in the waiting room. There's no need to fuss. I'm fine, just fine. I don't think I've been this good in a long, long time." Her voice trembled, and two tears trailed down her cheek.

"You must have heard from the lab. I don't want you to be sad—"

"Sad? Why, no. The reports came back negative. Negative!" More tears spilled down her beautiful face. "I don't know if I've ever been more grateful. My dear grandson is going to be just fine."

He closed his eyes. It wasn't cancer? It wasn't cancer. Relief washed through him, and he was afraid to believe it. But Nanna was crying again, big, happy tears. It was true. He was being given a second chance. A new beginning to his life.

Thank You, Lord.

One thing was for sure. He was going to keep the promise he made to God. Starting right now, this instant, he wasn't going to waste one more minute.

A woman knocked on the partly opened door, balancing two rather large florist arrangements. Word sure had gotten out about the "small procedure" he'd told his vice presidents about, and his attorney, just in case something had gone terribly wrong during surgery. Corporate gifts, no doubt, judging by the apparent cost of the arrangements.

"Please, excuse me. I'll just put these over here with the others," the friendly volunteer said as she crossed the room to the table, where way too many flowers had given their lives for him.

Maybe he'd have the nurses give the flowers to people on the floor who would enjoy them.

"Oh, this was obviously delivered to the wrong room, Mr. Ashton." The woman looked embarrassed as she pulled a single glass vase from the vast forest of flowers. "This couldn't be for you. I'll just take it out of your way."

It was a single white rosebud.

Julie. He knew it in a heartbeat, all the way down to his soul. He *hadn't* been dreaming. She *had* been here. Who else would have given him a single white rose?

"Wait. I want that. It's for me," he assured the woman, and she handed it over uncertainly.

The vase felt smooth and cool in his hand. The small white bud was closed tight, but it was perfect. There was no card because it had been delivered in person. He smelled the faint, faint scent of Julie's strawberry hand lotion on the vase.

Nanna patted at her tears with a cloth handkerchief she'd taken from her jumbo-size purse. "Hope told me that Julie brought that."

"She's here?" Play it cool, keep the excitement out of your voice.

"No, she went home. Heard you would be fine and said she had to go. Something about the annual food drive, but I didn't hear it all. She took out of here like a woman in a hurry." Nanna sounded innocent—she was very good at that. "Or like a woman with certain feelings for a certain man. Not that I'm one to name any names."

"Don't take so much pleasure in this," he told her, wincing when awful pain jackhammered through his midsection.

Julie left, did she? Now why would she fly halfway or more across the country just to deliver a single white rose? The same kind of flower he happened to buy her in Colorado?

What would have happened if he'd had the courage to tell her his true feelings on the flight back to Montana that day? And if he'd said those frightening words—*I love you.* Would she have turned away?

He'd been afraid then. But he wasn't afraid now. His past was gone, and he was a new man. And, being a goal-oriented, type A personality, he knew exactly what he wanted from life—Julie. She was the woman he intended to marry, who was going to have his children and, God willing, the woman he was going to grow old with.

His sister had found happiness, after sharing the same childhood. With God's help, so could he.

Chapter Fifteen

"Misty, you are a lifesaver," Julie said into the phone as she padded past the unlit Christmas tree in her living room, through the first meager splash of early-morning sun on the hardwood floor and went straight to the refrigerator. "I'm going to be indebted to you forever."

"Not forever. Only until my wedding reception, when I need someone to make sure everything goes without a hitch. Wanna guess who I'll call?"

"I think I already know." She grabbed the carton of hazelnut creamer and headed directly to the coffeepot.

She thanked Misty again, said goodbye and dug her favorite mug out of the cupboard. The big, double-size one. She needed caffeine and lots of it, enough to get her through the midmorning ceremony. This was her granddad's wedding day!

She savored that first sip, inhaling the rich coffee smell, enjoying the sweetness from the creamer, letting the warm liquid wake her up. Then the doorbell rang, shattering her perfect moment of peace.

She wasn't expecting anyone. Maybe it was Granddad. He could need help with his tie. He'd been a cowboy all his life, and not as experienced in tying ties as men who worked in offices. Like Noah.

Now, see how she'd gone and worked Noah into her thoughts? It just proved she wasn't as over him as she'd prayed to be. What was it going to be like seeing him today? He was supposed to be flying in this morning for the wedding. She wasn't sure how she felt about that. Only one thing was for sure—she was truly thankful he was healthy.

She yanked open the front door. A bouquet of white rosebuds—what had to be two dozen of them—was staring her in the face, practically obscuring the man holding the vase.

"Clifford? Is that you?" She could barely recognize the man who owned the local floral shop. "What are you doing with those? Wait—"

She could see past the enormous arrangement of flowers to the blue delivery van parked in her snowy driveway. The side door was wide open, revealing vase after vase of roses. Every single last one of them was white.

"Oh, no! Clifford, this is all wrong." She couldn't

believe it. And after all the care Nora had taken ordering the flowers. Julie should know—she'd gone with Nora and Hope to the florist regularly for the last two months.

"Sorry, Julie, but this order is correct. If you don't mind, I've got to get these delivered. I got a busy day ahead, as you know." Clifford sounded apologetic, yet determined.

Didn't he understand? "The roses are supposed to be blush pink. And why are you delivering them here? They have to go to the church."

"That's not what I have on my delivery slip." Clifford shouldered past her. "Where do you want these?"

"Back in your van." How could a mistake like this have happened? "Clifford, no, don't put them there."

"I told you, I've got a whole van to unload." He straightened, leaving the bouquet on her coffee table. "You sure don't seem very happy about this."

She was still in her sweats and slippers. How happy could she be? "Can I see the delivery order? I'm going to call Nancy. She'll get this straightened out for me."

"Don't bother, Julie. She'll agree with me." Clifford headed out the door, leaving it wide open as his assistant came in carrying two more bouquets.

Julie didn't understand. How could this be? She grabbed the phone, but the clerk who answered explained that Nancy wasn't available. She was at the church setting up for Nora's wedding.

"Well, that's it, then." Clifford edged the twelfth vase of white roses onto the edge of the end table. "Boy, aren't those something? That billionaire sure must think a lot of you."

"The billionaire? You mean Noah Ashton? He sent these?" She didn't believe it. "Clifford, come back here."

"Sorry. Got more flowers to deliver. See ya!" Clifford hopped off her porch as if his shoes were on fire.

Noah did *this?* She closed the door, turned around and slumped against it. Why would he send her twenty-four dozen roses?

The doorbell rang, and she jumped. Startled, she had the knob turning in her hand before she could think. There he was, standing on her porch, in a pair of worn jeans and a black wool coat, healthy and alive and strong. He looked completely recovered and entirely different from the vulnerable man lying in a hospital bed.

What was he doing here? She'd said goodbye to him. Closed her heart to him. Walked away.

And he dared to give her white roses, reminding her of their trip and how she loved him.

Pain shredded her heart. No, she wasn't going to do this. Pretend that an apology would make it okay, and they could be good friends again. Maybe he was hoping she'd take him skiing. Well, she didn't want to be his skiing buddy.

Mr. Noah Ashton would just have to go and torment someone else. She grabbed the door and gave it a hard shove. Something stopped her.

Noah's foot against the door frame. "If you close the door, then you're going to miss what I've come to say."

"Noah, I've got to get ready for the wedding."

"This won't take long. It's important. Please." He pushed open the door, gently, and walked into her home. Into her life. Into her heart.

"You can't come in here. I've got to—"

"Julie." He took her left hand in his, his grip tender, his touch warm, the deep affection in his voice as real as the floor at her feet. "I know you came to my hospital room, and I know why you didn't stay."

"You had your family there. You didn't need me, and I had to get back—"

"Julie." He brushed a kiss to her cheek, soft and surprising and gentle. "There's something I should have told you when we were standing on the mountain watching the sunrise. After I kissed you, I should have said, 'Julie, I love you.'"

"No." Tears burned her eyes. "You can't push your way in here and say you love me. You can't do that to me—"

"Sure I can. I brought flowers. I'm trying to make this right." His smile was genuine, his touch sure.

Right? Nothing could ever make her the same. She loved him, and now everything was different. What she wanted, what she needed. And he wanted a romance. Well, she didn't. She wouldn't lay her heart on the line for the wrong man, no matter how wonderful. How perfect.

To her horror he knelt before her, right there in her rose-scented living room, and pulled a black ring box from his pocket.

She stared at the small box that fit in the palm of his hand. No, this wasn't possible. He wasn't going to propose to her. He wouldn't be that cruel. Would he?

She started to back away, but her feet wouldn't move. Her mind was spinning so fast she couldn't object as he took her left hand in his.

"Julie, I love you." He was kneeling before her like a promise kept, steady and dependable.

No, this couldn't be real. She wouldn't believe it, even when she could see the hope in his dark, tender eyes. A horrible rushing filled her ears.

"Please," he asked sincerely, truly, "will you be my wife?"

"No!" How could he do this to her? Him and his jet and his twenty-four dozen perfect long-stemmed roses, and his billion-dollar bank account, or portfolio, or whatever it was rich men had. "You know I can't marry you."

"What?" He looked crestfallen.

That made it worse. She felt horrible and hopeless

and broken. She watched the great hope in his eyes fade increment by increment until only hurt remained, and she could see it deep. There was his heart, tender and true.

"What do you mean?" He sounded bewildered.

As if she'd simply leap at the chance to be a billionaire's wife, without looking to the future and to what really mattered. Anger ripped through her like a gigantic claw, leaving her feeling raw and torn apart. "I said no. I can't be your wife. Look at me."

"I'm looking." He stayed on one knee. "I see a beautiful woman, the only woman who has ever beaten me in a competition. The only woman I've been involved with who has kept her promises and never broken a trust. The one woman who stole my heart when I wasn't looking, and so I'm here before you, asking to spend the rest of my life with you. I truly love you."

"Stop saying that." How was she going to go on with her normal, ordinary life now? Once her grandfather's wedding was over and Noah flew on his shining white-and-gold jet back across the continent, how was she ever going to be able to pick her chin off the floor and pretend her heart wasn't shattered beyond repair? He loved her. That only made everything worse.

"Julie." He didn't move, gazing up at her with all those diamonds glittering against black velvet. "I know you love me. I know it. Don't you realize I'm on your side? That from now on, that's where I'm going to stand, and my feet are never going to stray. Where you go, I go. What you want, I want. We have love, and that's everything.''

"Sure, you say that now." She wrapped her arms around her middle, holding on tight, but she couldn't comfort herself. There was no comfort for this. "But what about in six weeks? Or maybe two minutes before the wedding?"

"What I say, I mean. You can always count on me, Julie. I will never hurt you like that. Never abandon you at the altar or anywhere else. Not after we're married. For better and worse, I'll be there for you." He stood, pulling her into his arms with such care. "I promise."

She buried her face in the soft wool of his jacket. She breathed in the scents of the spicy aftershave he always wore. She really loved that scent. She truly loved everything about this man. She was safe here, tucked against his chest, and it felt as if she belonged in his arms forever and ever.

It took all her courage to step away. "I drive a pickup. You travel in a jet. I don't see how this can work out. I wouldn't be happy in New York. Montana is my home. This is my community, where I belong. I teach the children here. I go to church here. My lifelong friends are here. My family is here. I can't leave, and you can't stay."

"I can't stay? I think I can. There's no law against it, is there?" He brushed her cheeks with his thumb, brushing away the tears she hadn't realized were there. "You know, I spoke to God before I came. He seemed to think Montana was a good place for me to be."

"Oh, right. For now. But you'll start missing your company and your friends and your apartment." She wanted forever. It wasn't possible. He couldn't see it, but she did. She'd been left at the altar. She had returned three engagement rings. How could she possibly give up Noah's ring?

"What if I told you I sold my company and the jet with it? You don't believe me, do you? Okay, well, I did. I also sold my apartment to my assistant, whom I promoted before I left. As for my friends, *you* are my best friend. Please, be my wife, too."

"I know you think you'll be happy here, and I'm sure you mean it now. But you're going to change your mind."

"Julie." His touch, gentle against her cheek. His kiss, as precious as a new day. "Just say yes, and let me prove it to you. I promise you that I am the one man who will never leave."

She *wanted* to believe him. She really did. She'd give almost anything to say the words he wanted to hear, the words she ached to say.

She couldn't marry him. This small-town life in rural Montana was the path the Lord had chosen for her. But it wasn't Noah's. How could it be? God had given him intelligence and brilliant business sense. Gifts that would go to waste here, where there were no giant corporations to run. Just modest hometown businesses that had been in families for generations.

She couldn't marry him. She refused to watch him grow restless and bored in a town that was too small for him.

Keep me on the right path, she prayed, as she opened the door and said the words she had to say. It was for his own good. And for hers. "Goodbye, Noah."

He snapped the ring box closed, clutching it in his fist. "No. I won't accept this. I hurt you by not saying this before. I won't do it by leaving you now."

"Staying would hurt me more. Just go." She set her chin, all fight, all determination. She was doing the right thing. It was that simple. "I mean it. I want you to leave."

He took a deep breath, as if the fight had gone out of him. His dependable shoulders slumped just a little as he marched past her. His boots knelled on her porch.

When he turned to face her, he was full of hurt. "I love you. You can push me away, but I'll keep coming back. Whatever it takes, I will prove to you that I'm here for now. For always."

He *would* make her believe it. He would show her the true depths of his commitment to her. One day she would see that she was his heart. And always would be.

Simple as that.

* * *

At the organ, Marj Whitly began the first strains of "Here Comes the Bride." "Aahs" broke out in the crowded church from the altar all the way to the back row at the first sight of the beautiful bride, draped in a light gray gown. On her arm was her grandson, James Noah Ashton the Third, in a dark gray tux.

"What a dream," Misty whispered, clinging to Julie's arm.

Exactly. Julie steeled her heart. That's what this morning had been. A dream. Surely nothing real, nothing that she ought to build her future on. Noah had been through a life-or-death experience, and he was naturally grasping at whatever he thought would make everything better. Yes, that was it. That's what he was doing by proposing to her. He was at a crossroads in his life, and he was making the choice he thought would bring him happiness.

She was making the right choice for both of them.

He looked so fine, with his dark hair tamed and the cut of the expensive suit perfectly fitted to his wide, muscular frame. No one could doubt the look of pride and love on his face as he escorted his grandmother down the aisle. Or the respect he showed when he gave the bride to her waiting groom.

Granddad. Julie ached with happiness for him. He looked dashing and dear, as he always did, even if he did fidget in the tight-fitting tux. Anyone could see the bride and groom were perfect for each other. Granddad's and Nora's love was the real thing.

Now and then fairy tales *did* happen.

When Granddad kissed his bride, the entire congregation applauded.

The sun chose that moment to smile through the stained-glass windows, casting bright hues over the bride and groom, as if to remind everyone in the church that love was God's greatest gift.

Time for plan B. *If* he could sneak out of the receiving line. Noah shook the mayor's hand, who planted his feet and looked about as hard to move as a cement barricade in the middle of a freeway.

"Mr. Ashton, pleased as punch to hear you're gonna be staying in our town. Prettiest piece that Montana has to offer. Well, we like to think so. After what you did, rescuing the little Corey girl from the creek, why, you're a member of this community already."

"Oh, yes, you may be from the big city," Mrs. Corey chimed from her place in line behind the mayor. "But you're one of us now."

Noah took the woman's words for what they were—a sincere compliment. He intended to live here, close to his grandmother, forever. And since Julie just happened to live here, well, didn't that work out perfectly?

"How are you holding up, son?" Harold asked, after the mayor had finally moved on and was shaking Nora's hand in congratulations. "I hear from my bride that you're still not up to snuff. Recovery takes time.''

"I'm fine." He still tired easily, but the fatigue was slowly improving, and he wouldn't let it stop him. He had a new chance at life, and he didn't intend to wait. He spotted Julie at the gift table, talking to his sister. Now would be the perfect chance to—

"Thanks for your confidence in me," Harold said, his voice gruff, looking down at his shoes. "I've done a fair job with my investments. I'll do even better with your grandmother's."

"I trust you." Harold was a good man. Okay, so Noah had been wrong—he could admit his mistakes. He knew without a doubt that Harold would treat his grandmother right.

"My dear grandson." Nanna caught him before he could break away from the crowd. "What a blessing you are to me. I'm so very thankful you are here with us today."

"You are a blessing to me, too, Nanna." He kissed her cheek. "Did I tell you what a beautiful bride you are?"

"Oh, my dear boy. It's so good to have you here." Nanna sparkled with happiness. "And as it happens, there goes Julie. I wonder where she's going? Maybe she could use some help with something. You had best go check, young man. Hurry along, now."

There was no fooling his grandmother.

Several people stopped him on the way to the door. To welcome him to town and to say that they sure appreciated how he helped out that day, which seemed so long ago now, when the little Corey girl needed help. He'd pitched in like a true Montanan, they said.

He brushed off their words, but appreciated their welcome. This little town was already beginning to feel like home. Now, if he could convince Julie of that, he'd be the happiest man on the planet.

He bolted out the door, but he couldn't see where she went. He tried the set of double doors that led outside. There was no sign of her in the snowy parking lot. The church, then? He strode down the hall, past the reception and into the quiet side entrance.

There she was, sitting in the front row, arms wrapped around her middle, gazing up at the sparkling stained-glass window. The giant cross glowed, as if God were giving him reassurance. This was the right path he was walking.

He gathered his courage, taking his time, searching for the right words. "The wedding was beautiful, wasn't it?"

She looked up, startled. She must have been lost in thought and didn't hear him approach. "It was lovely."

"*You* are lovely."

She covered her face with her hands. "I can't do this. Please just leave me alone."

"Why would I do that? The woman I plan to marry is hurting." He eased onto the bench beside her. "What can I say to make you believe?"

She bolted off the pew, her dress rustling around her. "Everyone is talking about how you're moving to town. Some say you'll stay. Others figure you'll be here for a few years, then head back to the city where you belong."

"And you think that's what I'll do. That a man who built a company that netted a half-trillion dollars in profits last year is someone who doesn't know what he wants. He can't make a good decision. He doesn't know where to invest his time and his effort."

"Maybe that man has had a scare, and he's evaluating his life. Maybe he's reaching for whatever will make him feel secure or happy."

"I have my faith for that. When I make a commitment, I mean it." He stood and gently turned her, so he could see the anguish on her face. "I love you truly."

"I love you, but I—"

"No buts." He kissed her gently, slanting his mouth over hers, letting her feel how he cherished her. "I've been unhappy for a long time. I want you to understand that. These changes I'm making aren't rash. I'm healthy and I'm grateful for it, and I realized when I woke up after my surgery that I had a debt to pay back to God. To live this life He has given me the right way, with love in my heart. I can't do that without you, Julie."

How could she believe him? How could she risk her heart this one last time? "No, I want a man who is right for me and my life. I want a marriage that lasts, not one torn apart by a midlife crisis or something when you decide you miss the excitement of a big city.''

''I see.'' He was patient, his touch loving as he traced her bottom lip with the pad of his thumb. ''Wasn't it you who said that the city was wasted on me? Julie, all I ever did was work. I'm tired of meetings and business trips and jet lag and irate attorneys yelling at me all day.''

''I can sympathize with those poor attorneys....''

There was the Julie he loved. The one who would keep his life interesting and keep him laughing. ''I want to be happy. I want to marry you.''

''You keep saying that.'' Tears filled her eyes, perfect, silver tears that shimmered and fell just for him to catch with his thumb.

''I'm going to keep saying it until you believe me. If it takes one thousand times, then fine. We have all day. If you need to hear it a million, then fine, the church has heat. We can stay here all night. But understand this. I'm never going to make you stand in front of that altar by yourself. I'm never going to make you regret saying the vows that will make us husband and wife.''

Julie's eyes were blurring, so it was hard to see the diamond ring when he slipped it on her hand. The band was cool platinum and as soft as a dream. The diamonds flickered and glittered like a thousand perfect rainbows. Promises that Noah intended to keep. He truly did love her.

Peace filled her, as gentle as the sunlight streaming through the windows, as reverent as the silence in the church. The candles glowed, and faint music lilted in from the reception room down the hall. God had led her here to this man and to this moment. She could *feel* it, deep in her soul.

"I'm standing here, in front of God, and I'm asking you again." He brushed away the last of her tears. "Will you marry me?"

"Yes." More joy than she had never known filled her, slow and sure, as Noah pulled her into his arms and kissed her long and tenderly.

Thank You, Lord, she prayed, burying her face in Noah's shoulder, holding him tight, holding him for keeps. They didn't need to speak. They stood in the peaceful sanctuary, with the sunlight and candlelight and their love that would last forever.

*   *   *   *   *

If you enjoyed
A LOVE WORTH WAITING FOR,
you will love Jillian Hart's
next inspirational romance
from Steeple Hill Love Inspired:
HEAVEN KNOWS
Available June 2003

Dear Reader,

When I was writing my first book for Steeple Hill Love Inspired, *Heaven Sent,* I fell in love with Hope's brother, Noah. I could sense in him a great loneliness, and I so wanted him to find his happily-ever-after. I was thrilled when I got the opportunity to tell his story. I expected a charming billionaire kind of a guy, and instead met a man of great faith, whose strength of spirit never wavered, even when facing uncertainty, pain and a possible terminal illness.

Noah reminded me of something important. Our time here is precious. There are blessings all around us in this incredible world. I hope you take the time out of your busy life to enjoy them in love and thanksgiving.

Jillian Hart

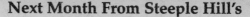